Get **more** out of libraries

Please return or renew this item by the last date shown.

You can renew online at www.hants.gov.uk/library

Or by phoning 0845 603 5631

Hampshire
County Council

Kendrick's Quest

The Civil War may be over but a lot of trouble remains. A shipment of California gold, collected to help the federal government's financial predicament, is ready for shipment to Washington D.C.

Former Union officer, Matt Kendrick, is sent to investigate the top-secret arrangements for shipping the gold and learns the hard way that someone has talked. With Kendrick now a target, he needs to contact whoever is carrying the information, but when murder piles on top of murder it's a tricky and deadly mission. That much gold helps to smoke out the greedy, but can Kendrick stop this attempt to help the South rise from the ashes of defeat?

Kendrick's Quest

J.D. Ryder

A Black Horse Western

ROBERT HALE · LONDON

© William Sheehy 2012
First published in Great Britain 2012

ISBN 978-0-7090-9963-5

Robert Hale Limited
Clerkenwell House
Clerkenwell Green
London EC1R 0HT

www.halebooks.com

Typeset by
Derek Doyle & Associates, Shaw Heath
Printed and bound in Great Britain by
CPI Antony Rowe, Chippenham and Eastbourne

CHAPTER 1

It's quite unlikely that one could get used to the rocking motion of a narrow gauge train, but it was that lurching that saved him.

The six-car train had stopped and a porter had placed a box on the platform so that travelers leaving the passenger car could step down. The big man, still a little off balance from the endless hours of being swayed one way then the other, was making that step when he stumbled and was just able to grab the door frame to keep from falling. Flung off balance, his body swung to one side and the thrown knife missed his broad chest, slamming into the side of the railcar.

For an instant all he could do was stare dumbfounded at the quivering blade, its point buried a good inch or more into the weathered wood paneling. Then, belatedly reacting, he jumped to the platform and, filling his hand with his Army issue Colt .44, stood crouched, ready for anything.

Matthew Kendrick's eyes quickly scanned the length of the empty dock. The elderly porter, his thin body frozen with fear and not taking his eyes off the Colt's wavering barrel, was the only person in sight. Across the platform the door to the waiting room was closed. Further down at the end of the loading dock, double doors to the baggage room were also shut tight. Kendrick ran to the end of the platform and looked past the station and up the dark, empty business street of the small

Nevada town. His attacker had escaped into the night.

The train trip had been memorable for being uncomfortable. After leaving Denver late in the afternoon, Kendrick had spent the last hours of daylight watching the countryside pass by a window. When darkness brought a halt to his sightseeing, he walked back to the sleeping car to see how he was going to fit in the fold-down bed of his compartment.

As he passed through the swaying passenger cars with their cracked leather bench seats filled with fellow travelers he was glad the colonel had paid for a private compartment. It was easy to see that sitting up in the car crowded with families, youngsters and all their baggage all around his six-foot long body, getting a good night's sleep wouldn't be possible.

After looking over the compartment that the colonel had reserved for him, Matt was almost sure his horse, riding in the stock car, was probably more comfortable. Standing better than six feet, the fold-down bed he was shown by the porter didn't promise many restful nights.

At long last he had reached his destination, Hunter's Crossing. Tired from not being able to get a good night's sleep, he was in a hurry to stand on something that didn't move. He was stepping off the train when the attack took place.

The knife was of a kind he hadn't seen many of and those that he had seen were usually in the possession of vaqueros working down in the Texas border country. About eight inches of thin steel tapering to a fine point and honed to razor sharpness on both sides and a short ivory handle. Balanced for throwing, it was clearly a knife that had been crafted for one thing only . . . to kill. Someone wanted Mama Kendrick's little boy, Matt, dead.

Nobody was supposed to know anything about him or the reason he was on this train. But someone did. There was no other reason for the attack. He was too new in the West to have made enemies. It had to have begun with Colonel Cummings and the proposed shipment of California gold.

Matthew Kendrick hadn't set out to work for Colonel Cummings, or for anyone for that matter. Agreeing to travel to Nevada to take delivery of some very private information seemed simple enough, and having just left his last employer, the US Army, he could use the money.

Colonel Cummings had assured the young man that the trip to Hunter's Crossing, Nevada, wasn't dangerous. Only if he let anyone in on what he was doing, the army officer had told him, would there be any threat. Well, he certainly hadn't mentioned his trip to anyone, but someone had. Somewhere in Hunter's crossing there was a killer.

CHAPTER 2

Beyond making sure he kept his horse and weapons, Kendrick hadn't thought too much about what was to happen after he resigned his army commission. Not long after one of the last battles of the Great War and the signing of General Lee's surrender, Kendrick had shucked his Union Army blue and gold uniform. He had had enough of the blood and gun smoke to last him a lifetime. At one time he had thought of making the army his life. The years he'd spent in uniform, fighting a war he didn't fully understand, had made him change his mind; a military career was not for him. All he wanted now was to get as far away from the war and its aftermath as he could.

The second son of a wealthy Boston family whose wealth came from importing various commodities, it was expected that he would, after attending a suitable university, take his place in the company.

As a youth he had known the day would come when he'd have to decide whether the East Coast business world would be what he wanted. Watching his father and older brother, he realized that commerce held little interest for him. One sun-filled morning, instead of joining the others in a discussion about the rights or wrongs of slavery, he signed up as an officer in the US Army. Now, after four years of college and another six wearing a uniform, he had discovered that a military career wasn't right for him either. Maybe whatever he was looking for was to be

8

found somewhere out in the West.

After saluting Colonel Cummings, his commanding officer, for the last time he had been invited to the colonel's tent for a drink.

'You were a fine officer, Kendrick,' the older man had commented as he poured a healthy amount of liquor into a pair of glasses. 'A fine officer and a good soldier. The army is going to need men like you in the coming months. The North may have won the war, but I don't think the last battle has been fought.'

Waving him to one of the folding chairs, the colonel went on talking. 'What exactly are your plans?'

Kendrick didn't want to say he hadn't thought that far ahead, so he sipped the fine whiskey before answering, giving himself time to think.

'Well, I think I'll start by heading out to California. The gold rush is about over, according to the newspapers, but there'll have to be a lot of opportunity out there for a young man.'

Neither spoke for a few minutes, merely relaxing and savoring the liquor. Matt Kendrick had drunk fine whiskey before, but he couldn't remember ever having tasted anything so smooth.

Finally Colonel Cummings put down his glass and looked at Kendrick. 'Maybe I can help out you a little. There's a job that needs to be done and I've been trying to find the right man to do it. . . .'

'That's generous of you, sir,' Kendrick interrupted. He finished his drink, stood up and placed the empty glass on a side table. 'But I just resigned my commission. I'm now a civilian.'

'Yes and that's why I think you'd be perfect for what I have in mind. Let me explain.' Ignoring the fact that the younger man was now standing, the colonel poured another three fingers of the smooth liquor into the empty glass before proceeding to describe the job.

The war might be over, the colonel explained, but the next few months were going to be hard on the victorious government.

Paying off most of the army now that the soldiers were no longer needed, setting up all the programs to start rebuilding both the North and South, would take a lot of money. Funding a war such as this one had almost depleted the government's war chest. That was where Kendrick came into the picture.

'The war and then Lincoln getting killed caused a lot of problems for the man who replaced him,' the colonel said when the two men had taken chairs on the hotel porch. 'When Andrew Johnson took over the office, he found that the government was about bankrupt. There are many in Congress who are hoping Johnson's government will fall because of this. The Confederation might have lost the war, but the Union could easily lose the peace.'

'How does this affect me? It was the politics of things that caused me to leave the Army,' Matt said, 'and I don't want to get involved with any secret spy deals.'

'No. What I need you for is not spying. I need someone who is not known. A group of California businessmen are putting together a load of gold bullion. That gold will take the pressure off our president.'

Colonel Cummings went on to explain just what he was asking Kendrick to do. He wouldn't, he was assured, have anything to do directly with the shipment itself. The businessmen would get it to a place called Hunter's Crossing, Nevada, and the government would have to take it from there. Kendrick's job would be to act as the go-between, meet with the Californians' representative and learn when and how the shipment was being made.

'They seem to want to meet face to face with our man,' Cummings said. 'I suppose it's all about seeing if we can be trusted to get the bullion on to Washington DC. That's why I've been looking for just the right man, someone who is honest and trustworthy and looks it. That describes you perfectly, I'm happy to say.'

When Kendrick had acquired the information, it would be

telegraphed back to the colonel in a special code he'd be given. The colonel would then set things in motion to transport the gold on to Washington. For this little service Kendrick would be paid $500.

'Five hundred dollars? That's quite a sum for doing no more than acting as a go-between. How do you know I won't try to steal the gold myself?'

'Oh, I know quite a bit about you. I've had my eye on you since you first mentioned your plan to take off the uniform. Let's see, you are thirty years old, from an honorable family and have been formally educated,' Colonel Cummings said, as if reading from a paper. 'Your time in the Army earned you various commendations, more were won during the recently concluded Great War, or as some call it, the Civil War. There was nothing, I'd say, civil about it, but there you are.' Watching, he saw that Matt was not impressed with his research. 'I tell you so you'll know I am not wrong. I do know all I need to know.'

Frowning into his now empty glass, the colonel went on. 'OK, let me get on with it. I have some contacts with people high up in government in Washington, DC. There is a lot of interest there in the West. Even before the end of the war, President Lincoln had directed that the railroads be employed to open up the country to settlement. That action was to do two things; first as a benefit for the men who would be coming home after the war. Yes, I see your surprise. But the leaders knew that the end was coming, and that there would be a need for those men and their families to make their new home.'

Colonel Cummings poured himself another inch or so of the whiskey and went on with his lecture. 'The second reason was to tie this country together. There are people in Mexico who have hopes of taking back California and those other areas they lost. Plus, both Russia and Great Britain have plans. A continental railroad system would close all those doors.'

Matt's frown deepened. 'Those political men in the capitol can make their plans all day long, but those plans don't have anything to do with me. I'm just an unemployed former solder on his way to something somewhere.'

'Yes, I know. A captain in the Michigan Regulars. Just having resigned and now, even before you've got around to packing a bag, here I am trying to recruit you again.

'Now don't think we aren't careful. We are. The gold shipment will be protected until we get it and afterward as well. You won't see the shipment. I can't send just anyone but, from your record, I believe you're probably the best man I've seen for taking on the job.'

Colonel Cummings set aside his glass, and took a paper from an inside pocket. 'This ticket will take you to Hunter's Crossing,' Colonel Cummings explained, 'the last stop on the west side of Nevada before the mountain range. Cattle pens are being built there, and stock from California as well as Nevada will use it as a shipping point. Those herds of cattle will be sent by rail east to the bigger markets. That's where you'll meet up with the Californian representative. We don't know who that'll be but we've been assured he will find you.'

Familiar as he was with the Army's long-term plans, Matt knew something about the importance of rail traffic. The system of railroads that had been constructed in the Northern states had been a big factor in the Union's success in winning the Great War. Being able to move all kinds of raw materials to one manufacturing center or another changed that part of the nation from depending on agriculture. Industry, both heavy and light, meant jobs and brought new wealth to a growing population. Railroads also helped open up new parts of the country, bringing families and their household goods farther west before putting it all on a wagon for the final push into the new land.

The former officer had read about the coming of the connection that was to link up the eastern seaboard with the far west coast, but that final tie had only just been made. The news was in all the newspapers, about the big ceremony in which the golden spike had been driven, linking up the Union Pacific and Central Pacific railroads. The rails coming from the east had met up with those laid across California, up and over the mighty Sierra Nevada mountains.

Matt had heard all about the struggle it took to make the trip in the dead of winter. Long before rails had been laid, and even before the gold rush of 1849, there had been stories of entire wagon trains loaded down with pioneers being lost in the mountain passes in winter. Now the railroad people were telling everyone they would soon be able to make the trip in comfort.

That was the job he'd taken on and nobody else was to know that he wasn't just another traveler heading west. It was unlikely, though, that someone would want to stab a simple traveler heading for a cattle-shipping point. Someone knew as much as he did about what he had gotten into. With a couple more days and nights to spend on the train, he'd have to keep his eyes open.

CHAPTER 3

'There will be hell and damnation, if those people are allowed to come into town.'

The Reverend Caleb Neely, for all his holy demeanor, came close to using strong language, Sheriff Morgan Blanchard thought, the kind more likely coming from a mule skinner, when told no. Worse, it wasn't just no, but an unrelenting denial.

The two men had met on the board sidewalk just down from the biggest and best hotel in Hunter's Crossing. Blanchard might have been looking at the preacher eye to eye, both men being tall; there the resemblance ended. The sheriff was broad shouldered in his dark woolen suit, while Neely was as thin as a rail.

'Damn it all to hell, Reverend,' the lawman responded tiredly, 'the answer is the same as it was yesterday and the day before that . . . no!' Glancing up the street toward a few others walking on the sidewalk, he pointed a finger at them. 'The cattle buyers and cattlemen are already starting to arrive. They will negotiate over the next couple of days and by the time you hold your Sunday services most will have either taken the train back East or ridden to their home place. They won't be here long enough to raise the kind of trouble you're talking about.'

Holding on to his temper, the preacher fought to soften his voice. 'Sheriff, you of all people in this community should

14

understand the harm these people can cause. Maybe not the ones coming in this week. They are only the beginning of what will come. Once the buyers and those with beef to sell get together, it'll only be a matter of time before the cattle drives will begin. That means that men who have been on the trail for long periods of time will be arriving. You know as well as I that when they get the opportunity they'll just naturally want to cut loose. And it'll be here, in our town, that they'll do it.'

'Reverend Neely, I sympathize with you. But there are others in this town who look forward to the hard cash those men will bring in.' Raising his voice to overcome the tall pious-looking man's instant response, the badge-toter went on. 'Along with the cattle buyers who will be filling up the hotel and eating in the restaurant, there's the money spent at the railroad. Now, you get all those folks to agree to turn those cattlemen away and I'll listen. Until then,' he continued, shaking his head as the red-faced preacher sputtered, knowing he had lost the battle, 'stop coming to me with your demands every chance you get. There is nothing I can do.'

'What you mean is there is nothing you *will* do.' Neely was a tall, thin man with a long narrow face made longer by his untrimmed beard. Keeping with his stern, hard appearance, his long thin nose was all that separated small black eyes set too close together. Unforgiving, the town's preacher saw gloom and doom coming on the heels of the building of loading pens down where the new railroad station was going up.

'Sheriff,' he warned, not stopping long enough to take a breath, 'the good people of this town won't forget this. There will be an election and we will remember the side you took in this matter.' Having got in the last word, Reverend Neely turned and, with shoulders shaking with anger, stomped on down the plank sidewalk.

The sheriff stood shaking his head and watched the preacher walk away.

'I couldn't help overhearing,' said a gentle voice. Caught

unawares, the sheriff glanced over his shoulder and found two older men and a young woman standing a few feet behind him. The men were both dressed in dark broadcloth suits and black string ties. One was short and stocky and the other taller and probably a little older. The older of the two had the look of a tired man, his shoulders permanently slumped. His eyes, buried deep under thick black eyebrows, looked dark and hidden. Holding a stained, worn felt hat in one hand, after glancing up at the sheriff he let his gaze slide away.

From the sunburned washboard-wrinkled skin of his face, the sheriff thought it likely that he had behind him a lifetime of working outdoors in the California sun. Halfway up his forehead, where the sun or wind had not got to because of a wide-brimmed hat, the skin was almost pasty white.

The shorter man had a more pleasant face, open and smiling. His bowed legs attested to a lot of time having been spent in the saddle. The sharp points of black cowboy boots peeked out from the bottoms of his pants. His Stetson was also black but somehow softer looking than his friend's. Probably newer, Morgan thought, noticing the wide hatband circling the crown, which was decorated with small silver discs, marking the wearer as a man with pride in his appearance.

From the way the man stood protectively beside the girl, it was clear that the pair were father and daughter. Where his hair was streaked with gray, her long black hair gleamed in the warm summer sun. Morgan Blanchard had always been easy around women and appreciated their beauty. This young lady, while not a classic beauty, was blessed with big dark brown eyes that she knew how to use. As he watched, he noted how she looked directly at the sheriff, not letting her eyes waver. That habit, he knew from experience, would make most men uncomfortable. She was obviously a woman used to the outdoors: the skin on her face was smooth and well-tanned, setting off her natural red lips. Morgan judged her to be about twenty years old and unmarried. Father and daughter were a happy pair, the smiles on both their faces spread far beyond their lips, bringing a sparkle to their eyes.

'We couldn't help our eavesdropping, Sheriff,' the young woman said.

'And,' her father quickly added, 'I suspect we are part of the cause for that man's anger. We're among those here to negotiate the proposed cattle drive that your friend seems to be against. My name is Harcourt, Clarence Harcourt, and this is my daughter, Susan. Old sourpuss here is our neighbor and the best friend anyone could have. Joad Howard's operation borders on to ours and both are backed up by the American River, over near Sutter's Fort on the other side of the mountains. We came over on the Central Pacific to find out about shipping our beef on that new railroad,' he finished, putting out his hand.

'Yep,' Blanchard smiled and shook the offered hand, 'you ranchers, along with the buyers coming in from the East, have got some of the town folks all up in arms. I'm the local sheriff, Morgan Blanchard, and that was our preacher, Reverend Caleb Neely. He was letting me know the world will be coming to an end if this becomes a shipping point for cattle.'

Susan Harcourt's smile grew. 'I certainly hope that isn't the way everybody here views it.'

'No. Not by a long shot. Having the railroad choose to put the station here will make this community grow, but that growth is seen by some folks as being a disaster. Personally, I think the good reverend is afraid some other preacher will come in and give his harsh, full-of-thunder Sunday sermons some competition.'

Harcourt laughed. 'We all took rooms in the hotel, Sheriff. Possibly you would take supper with us later today?' the rancher asked, taking his daughter's arm.

'Well, that's kind of you. But my wife, Claire, wouldn't let me hear the end of it if I didn't invite you to our house for the meal. The restaurant does serve good food, but, well, you know how women are.'

Susan looked at her father and Howard and, getting a nod from both, agreed. 'We would be pleased to accept your invitation,' she said with a smile. 'Uncle Joad and Father and I have spent the last three days on the train in each other's company. It would be good to talk with another woman for a change.'

'Good. I'll tell Claire to expect you, say, just about sundown? Our place is over in the next block,' Blanchard said, pointing, 'you can't miss it. We've got the only white picket fence along that street.'

The three nodded their agreement and walked back toward the hotel. Sheriff Blanchard turned and ran into a man who had just stepped out of the hotel's entrance. Flustered at the near collision, he stopped and watched as the man bent over to pick up his hat, which had been knocked off by the collision.

Taken aback, Blanchard blurted his question. 'I suppose you're another cattleman or,' he frowned and took another look at the man who now stood, brushing off his hat, 'no, I'd say you're more likely a cattle buyer.'

'Neither,' Matt Kendrick laughed as he brushed off his hat. 'Just a traveler. Arrived on the train and nearly got run over.' Amused by the look on the sheriff's face, he quickly went on, 'No harm done, though.'

After arriving on the morning train, Matt had unloaded his horse, settled the big animal in the town's only stable, and checked in to the hotel. Leaving his carpetbag in the room, he had decided to look the town over, and literally ran into the town's lawman.

Mollified and past his surprise, the sheriff nodded his acceptance at the stranger's words, taking his time looking the newcomer over. What he saw was a tall, broad-shouldered man standing in a loose-jointed way. Something about him, though, suggested that if necessary, he could be dangerous. The Colt, holstered butt forward on his left side wasn't there to shoot the odd snake in the trail. No sir, from his brief experience of wearing a badge, the sheriff had quickly learned the difference between a gun worn for show and one worn by someone who was serious about its real use.

'I suppose I should do the apologizing,' he said, keeping his face expressionless. 'I'm only a little touchy.'

Matt chuckled. 'Well, no damage done. It isn't the best way to make the acquaintance of the town's law, though.'

Relaxing a bit, Blanchard smiled.

'My name's Matt Kendrick. I'm just traveling through, on my way to California and thought I'd stop for a day or two, get a night's sleep in a bed that's a little longer than the one on the train.' Having stated his name, he was about to offer his hand when a handful of younger men came rushing up, breaking into the two men's conversation.

'Sheriff, it is not right,' the obvious leader all but shouted, ignoring Matt. 'My father is about to explode because you won't listen. This is our town and we like it the way it is. Your letting those cattlemen and their rowdy hired hands take over will put the rest of us in danger. You have to do what is right and stop it.'

The young men were all of an age, most looking to Matt to be in their early twenties. The leader, a slender but well-built young man with a full head of red hair, was nearly as tall as the sheriff. His face was angular, but had a soft quality that denoted his youth. Blue eyes, made more noticeable by the paleness of his skin, glared at the lawman.

Standing behind the young speaker, the others were silent but very much supportive of their leader.

'Jonathan,' Sheriff Blanchard said, letting his anger show, 'I'll tell you what I told your pa. There is nothing I can do to stop this from happening. The railroad has decided that Hunter's Crossing is centrally located. This attempt at getting ranchers and buyers together is something like a test. Those folks I was talking to just now were among the first passengers to come over the mountain on the railroad. Yes, if it works, this will become a much more important community. Passenger and freight trains traveling in either direction can take on water and wood here. All that means the town will be changing and there is nothing that can be done about that.'

'There must be something,' one of the other young men said, almost as loudly as the preacher's son. This man, smaller of build than the preacher's son, had dark blond hair which he wore long, stood slightly to one side and a little behind him. The men, Matt noticed, were wearing almost identical clothes, almost like a uniform: pinstriped wool pants, white shirts and flat-soled laced shoes, typical of a town businessman. Looking at the others, he saw that most of them were similarly dressed.

'All this will destroy all the work our parents have put in to make this a good, God-fearing town,' the blond haired young man declared.

'Go home, boys. Go home,' Sheriff Blanchard said, shaking his head in disgust. 'Having a few cattlemen come this week isn't going to cause any damage to the town. Go home.' Nodding once again at Matt Kendrick, who had stepped back and was leaning against an awning pole, the lawman turned and walked away.

Ignoring the man standing under the overhang, the young men muttered among themselves for a few minutes, then, as one, they turned and walked away in the other direction, to disappear beyond the hotel.

CHAPTER 4

Hunter's Crossing was a small town but with plenty of room for the expected growth. With the work on the cattle pens proceeding at a good pace, that growth had actually already started. Until the announcement had been made that the junction with the western terminus was to be here, the one hotel had been enough. Now there were two others being built, each with its own restaurant and saloon.

For a long time Hunter's Crossing had been no more than a place for travelers from the East going to the goldfields of California to have a place to rest before climbing the high Sierras and then going on into California. Located on the old emigrant trail, the town was backed up against the foothills of the Sierras on one side and the Nevada desert on the other.

The town's business street ran east and west, starting at the stone bridge across the Truckee River at one end, on to the last of the false-fronted buildings that lined both sides of the main street at the other. A series of smaller streets branched off on either side. Along these were the houses where the local citizenry lived. Most had been built of sawmill lumber and, if painted, were either white or barn red. On the main street, only the bank and the courthouse, including the sheriff's office, had been built of stone, the rest were of milled lumber, nearly all of them single story made to appear higher by the false fronts. Signs announcing the various businesses hung out over the sidewalks that lined both sides of the thoroughfare.

Until the railroad came, maintaining the law in Hunter's Crossing had been easy. Twice a day Blanchard walked through the town, tipping his hat to people and stopping to talk when the opportunity presented itself. He had been appointed to the job the previous winter, when the elected sheriff, old James Hunter, died suddenly. The old man had been the last of the pioneering family that had originally started the small settlement. The town's doctor said the sheriff's death was from pneumonia, and there was nobody to dispute that. Morgan and Claire Blanchard had recently moved into town and Morgan had been thinking about opening up a lawyer's office when he was asked to take on the job of sheriff, at least until an election could be held. The city's leaders wanted to wait until the railroad was running to see what effect that would have on the town before holding the election.

Up to now, it had been a quiet town, but Morgan Blanchard was sure that that would change with the coming of the railroad. He'd seen it happen before. As he was thinking about what it could mean his thoughts were interrupted by loud yelling up the street behind him. Turning back, he saw a small crowd of people in front of the hotel.

Holding his holstered belt gun from bouncing against his leg, the sheriff trotted toward the milling crowd. As he drew closer he heard loud young voices yelling taunts at someone.

'No,' he heard one voice call out as he reached the outer edges of the crowd. 'That won't do any good. Let me talk with these people. Stop crowding them.'

The single voice was drowned out by others. It was apparent that the town's young men had found a target. Sheriff Blanchard was stunned to see the rancher, Harcourt, and his daughter at the center of the mob.

'Let me through,' he growled, pushing against the dozen or so yelling and cursing members of the gang. 'Come on, break it up and move on.'

The shouting grew louder as Blanchard pushed and shoved against the crowd. At last, in disgust, he pulled his six-gun, pointed it at the sky, and pulled the trigger. At the same instant he heard the girl scream.

Blanchard pushed through and saw the young girl lying on the ground. The big newcomer, Kincaid, was kneeling next to her, holding her head up. His body and one arm, swinging first one way and then the other, were protecting her from the surging mob of men, mostly young, but a few of riper years, who were fighting. After taking a quick glance at the jam-packed mass of men, the sheriff used the barrel of his revolver and started cracking heads.

Swinging down hard, right and left, he dropped three men and, ready to continue, stopped only when he found himself to be the only man standing. Most of the others that'd been in the crowd had fled and those remaining were, for the most part, either lying in the dust of the street or were on their hands and knees.

The street was suddenly quiet as the sheriff took time to eject the empty shell from his six-gun. He reloaded and shoved it back in the holster before turning back to where he'd last seen the rancher's young daughter.

'If you're looking for that pretty girl, Sheriff, that big stranger carried her off,' a bystander said. 'Took her off over there,' the man pointed, 'on the boardwalk by the general store.'

Blanchard quickly looked over those men who were still in the street and waved to the bystander. 'See if you can get these bums out of the street, will you?' he called. 'Someone should probably go see if they can find Doc Moser.'

Both the newcomer and Susan Harcourt were sitting on the boardwalk, the girl placed so she could lean against a porch post.

'She's all right,' the big man said, seeing the concern in the lawman's face. 'Just had the wind knocked out of her by those idiots.'

Blanchard stood over them, shading Susan's face from the late afternoon sun. Her once white shirtfront was now covered with dirt from the street, and smudges of dust powdered the left side of her face.

'We should get her to the hotel,' the sheriff said, 'I lost track of where her pa got off to in that mob, but it's certain he'll be worried about her.'

'Yeah,' Matt said in agreement.

Slowly, taking a series of deep breaths as if to fill starved lungs, the young girl started showing some signs of life. Abruptly, she sat up with and, after a few minutes of looking around dazedly, came fully awake. Looking from man to man, she scanned the near-empty street.

She sounded distressed as she asked, 'Where's my father?'

CHAPTER 5

Sheriff Blanchard shook his head. 'I didn't see where he went, ma'am, I lost sight of him in that crowd. He probably made his way on over to the hotel.'

'He was right beside me when those young men came running up yelling at us. He shoved me behind him and I got knocked down when they grabbed at him. I heard a shot and . . . where is he? Is he all right?' Her face went pale as both men shook their heads.

'He wasn't in the street when I got there,' the sheriff said. 'And that shot was into the air. Just to get everyone's attention.'

'I didn't notice your pa, ma'am,' Matt said. 'But then I don't know what he looks like. When I saw you on the ground I pushed through to protect you. Those fools weren't looking and would have trampled you. But I didn't see anyone who looked like he could be your father.'

'Father,' she called, shakily coming to her feet, her eyes searching the length of the street. 'Sheriff, you have to find my father.'

'First thing is to get you inside.' Looking at Matt, the sheriff frowned, 'Will you help her over to the hotel while I see to those men I had to buffalo? Miss Susan, I'm sure you'll find your pa at the hotel.'

'Certainly,' Matt said, putting out a hand to help steady the girl.

Still looking a little dazed, she took his hand, then looked up at him. 'I'm sorry, but we haven't met, have we?'

'No, ma'am, we haven't. I'm Matthew Kendrick, Matt to my friends.'

'OK, Mr Kendrick. My name is Susan Harcourt, and thank you for helping me.'

Offering her his arm for support, Matt walked the girl across the street and into the hotel lobby. Not finding anyone behind the counter, Matt asked her which rooms she and her father had and looked to see if the numbered key was on its peg. He didn't comment on not finding the key hanging on the board. It seemed likely that if her pa had come to the hotel he would have already been in the rooms.

He unlocked the door to the room for her, stepped aside and let her rush in, calling out for her father. Her room and the one adjoining were empty.

Matt, holding his wide-brimmed hat in one hand, watched as panic once more filled the young woman.

'Ma'am,' he said, taking her arm and leading her to a chair. 'You're in no condition to go rushing out. Rest yourself and I'll go see what I can find.'

'I had better go along with you,' she said, attempting to stand up.

'No. You've been shaken up. Sit here for a bit and I'll go. You rest and wait. I'll come back as soon as I find him.'

The main street was quiet and empty when Matt started his search. Seeing the sheriff down the street, he headed in that direction.

'Hey, Sheriff,' he called as the lawman started into a building. 'I left Miss Harcourt in the hotel. Did you see her pa?'

'He wasn't at the hotel? Damn, where could he have got off to?' Pointing on up the street, he scowled. 'You head on that way. He could have been hurt and taken on up to the saloon or maybe the doctor's office. I'll search down toward the river.

He's a short man, wearing a dark suit and riding boots. Plain as day, he's a cattleman.'

'All right, I'll meet up with you,' Matt said as he walked away. He stopped at every door as he made his way up the street, opening each one and looking everywhere. At the saloon, he stepped to one side of the double doors and let his eyes adjust to the dim light. In one corner a half-dozen or so young men, the young red-headed preacher's son among them, looked up as he stepped into the darkened room. Silently they watched him as he searched for the older man.

'I'm looking for a short man,' he softly called to them, recognizing most as being in the group that had been led by the preacher's son. 'A cattleman, I'm told. Probably the man you brave gentlemen attacked out in the street. He's gone missing. Any idea where he might have gotten off to?'

Nobody said anything for a minute. 'A cattleman,' one of the seated men said in a loud voice. 'It's those kind of people we don't want in our town.'

'So you attack the old man and his daughter out in the street? If that's the way you treat guests to your fine community, maybe this place isn't worth coming to. Now, I'll ask again,' letting his voice grow hard, 'did any of you brave men see where he went?'

'No,' came the answer after a minute or two.

Matt shook his head in disgust and went back out on the street. On finding the doctor's office empty he continued to the end of the street before coming back down the other side.

Sheriff Blanchard was standing in front of his office talking to two men when Matt finished his search.

'No sign of him and I didn't find anyone who saw what happened, Sheriff,' he said as he walked up.

'Not down that way, either,' the sheriff said. He pointed to the two men and went on, 'These men have just come into town and have offered to help us look. They are more of the cattlemen expected to meet up with the buyers.'

'I'm Ivan Russo,' the younger of the two said, sticking out his hand. 'We've got a spread up north a piece. Heard about the proposal to ship cattle east by rail and thought I'd come down to see what kind of offer the buyers would make. Sheriff here says another cattleman was attacked and has turned out to be missing.'

Matt took the offered hand and looked the man over. Not as young as he had first thought, probably only a few years younger than his own thirty years. Dressed like the cattleman he was, Russo wore his black pants tucked into high-topped riding boots. A black cloth vest was worn over a long sleeved cotton shirt. A brightly colored bandanna was tied around his neck. The rancher's face was long with high cheekbones. Full lips were curved into a smile that somehow, Matt noticed, didn't reach the man's eyes. Eyes which were hard as he returned the inspection.

Standing silently beside Russo, a second man smiled a little at Matt's scrutiny of the rancher. He was older and dressed in a flashier style. His black Stetson was shaped with care, its wide brims rolled to each side. His white shirt was made whiter-looking by contrast with the black wool pants that hung outside his dusty black sharp-toed riding boots. Small silver conchos decorated his gunbelt and the holster that held a bone-handled six-gun, butt forward on his left side. Not moving, he didn't offer his hand or a name.

'Forgive me,' Russo said, quickly, 'this is Grogan, my ranch foreman. He and another hand came down with me. We just got into town. Barnwell is taking care of our horses. Now, how can we help in this search?' He turned back to the sheriff.

Once again, under the direction of the sheriff, the town was searched. The four men spread out and every building was gone through. As the sun was setting Blanchard called the search off and went to give Susan Harcourt the bad news.

CHAPTER 6

Sheriff Blanchard found Matt in the restaurant having breakfast the next morning. The lawman ordered a cup of coffee as he sat down across from the cowboy.

'Any sign of the missing rancher this morning?' Matt asked.

'Not a trace. We had Susan Harcourt over at the house for dinner, but she was too worried to eat much. Claire, my wife, insisted that she stay with us last night. We have a spare bedroom. It's supposed to be for a baby, but we haven't made any yet. Anyhow, I don't think any of us got much sleep.'

When the breakfast dishes were taken away the two men were relaxing with a second cup when the street door crashed open and a young boy came running in.

'Sheriff, you gotta come down to the river,' the boy was yelling in his excitement. 'Me and Roy found a dead man.'

Hurrying to keep up with the running boy, the two men were told how the boys, fishing in the river that morning, had seen something caught in the willows below the bridge. The two boys had waded out into the water a little, until they could see the back of the man's head.

'Do you think he drowned?' the boy, whose name, Matt learned, was Sammy, asked two or three times. 'I ain't never seen a dead man before.'

On reaching the river they found the second boy sitting silently on the bank, staring at the water. 'He was turning in the water and I got scared he'd float on away so I took that stick and pulled him in,' the other boy, Roy, said quietly. 'I didn't want to touch him. I ain't never touched no dead man before.'

The body, wearing only long-handled underwear, was face down, bobbing gently in the backwash of the river. Blanchard sat on the bank and pulled his boots off before wading into the water. He took a hold of the gray-white cloth covering the man's back and pulled the body to the bank, where Matt helped by grabbing an arm. The two boys stood near by, not wanting to miss anything but far enough away to take off running, if it came to that.

Once the body was out of the water the sheriff turned it over and exclaimed. 'Ah, damn.'

Without being told, Matt knew it had to be the missing cattleman, Harcourt.

'Boys,' Sheriff Blanchard said, trying to keep the boys from seeing too much, 'you run up to get Doc Moser, will you. Don't go stopping anywhere or telling anyone what we've got here. That'll be my job and I'll be mighty mad if you don't do what I say.'

Proud to be given such an important job and happy to get away, the boys raced off.

'I wanted them gone. See this?' the sheriff asked, pointing to the side of the dead man's head where a flap of torn scalp partially covered a blood-darkened bruise. 'Looks like he'd been hit in the head before being tossed into the river.'

'Wonder where his clothes are?' Matt asked. 'You don't think he was killed for his pants and boots, do you?'

'No, and I don't reckon he had much cash money on him either. However,' Blanchard sat back on his heels, and dried his hands on his pants leg and shook his head, 'I guess there are those who'd kill a fella for a few dollars.'

'What about all that yelling on the street yesterday? Were those young men angry enough to carry out their threats?'

Blanchard frowned. 'I don't want to think that's what happened. These are good people. They're just scared about what they see as bad times coming.'

They watched as a portly man, his short legs pumping fast to keep up with the youngster who had him by the hand came running down the street. From the worn black doctor's bag he carried, the leather cracked and scuffed, Matt figured he would be the doctor the sheriff had sent for.

After waiting a moment to catch his breath the doctor gave the dead body a cursory look while the boy, Sammy, excitedly explained why his friend had run home. 'Roy was scared,' the boy said proudly. 'I did what you said and didn't tell anyone. I wasn't scared even a little bit.'

'Well, Sammy, that's pretty brave of you,' Sheriff Blanchard said, placing a hand on the boy's shoulder. 'But now we have to let Doc Moser do his work and he can't do that with everybody standing around. You go on home and tell your ma where you've been. But remember, don't tell anyone about what you boys found, hear me?'

Disappointed, and looking back over his shoulder as he slowly walked back into town, Sammy did as ordered.

'Looks like it's too late to be calling me for this fellow,' the short, stubby doctor, who obviously lived well, said as he kneeled next to the body. As the sheriff had done earlier, he pointed to the wound on the dead man's head.

Blanchard agreed. 'Yeah, I didn't figure there'd be much you could do for him, but I thought you could tell us how he died. That was before we turned him over and saw that wound on his head. Is that what killed him, or did he drown after all?'

Moser, glancing up at Matt, motioned to him. 'Help me turn him over on his stomach.'

After the dead man had been rolled over Matt and the sheriff watched aghast as the doctor straddled the body and, with his hands placed on either side of the dead man's lower back, pressed hard a few times.

'Nope,' the rotund man said, standing up and brushing off the knees of his pants. 'I'd say he didn't drown. Wasn't no water in his lungs. Probably killed for whatever he had in his pockets. There are a lot of strangers in town, you know.'

'This is one of those "strangers", Doc,' Blanchard said. 'The dead man and his daughter have a cattle ranch over on the California side of the mountains.'

Doc Moser looked up at the two men and nodded. 'There's likely to be more of this happening because of them kind coming here, too,' he said. 'The Reverend Neely warned us this would happen.'

The sheriff scowled at the professional man and turned to Matt. 'You mind keeping an eye on him while I go get a wagon? I'll have him taken up to the undertaker's and then go tell the girl that we found her father. This is going to be rough on her.'

CHAPTER 7

After leaving Harcourt's body with the undertaker the sheriff and Matt were walking back down the main street when someone in the alley next to the hotel hailed them. They changed direction and found Russo and his foreman standing over another man who was sitting in the dirt, leaning up against the building. Even from ten feet away, Matt could smell the strong odor of liquor. A whiskey bottle lay on its side a few feet from the sitting man's feet. That man sat holding his head.

'This is my hired hand,' Russo told the sheriff. 'We found him here, stinking like a . . . I don't know what. Drunken fool. When I said something about our spending our time searching for that cattleman last night while he was off getting drunk, he said he'd heard something about that.' Kicking the sitting man's foot, he snarled an order. 'Go on, tell the sheriff what you told us.'

'Ah, gawd, my head hurts,' the man said, clutching his head even more tightly. Long straggly black hair hung loose and limp over his face, half-hiding his bony nose and chin, which was covered with a three-day beard.

'Damn you, Barnwell. This is more important than your head. Tell the sheriff what you heard.'

Moving his head slowly, as if it would break, the seated man looked up with one eye open at the men standing over him. Then he groaned again, quickly closed that eye and let his head

33

drop. 'Last night. It was over in the saloon. Musta been late. I couldn't find you guys, boss, so I stopped for a drink. Figured you'd come in sooner or later. I was standing at the bar, talking to some fella there. He left after a little while and I was alone.'

'We don't care about that, Barnwell. Tell us what you said you heard,' Russo demanded, kicking at the man's foot again. The drunken man's clothes showed signs of having been slept in, his shirt, sun-bleached and faded with a pocket half torn off, was partly pulled out of his pants and dirt streaked a pant leg. The boot that the rancher was kicking was well worn and scuffed; a hole in the sole of the other showed the dirty sock the man was wearing.

'OK, OK. It was a bunch of young punks, sitting over against the wall. They were arguing about something. One of them sounded real mad. He said something about knowing what needed to be done, then he stomped out. The others sat for a while talking and then they all left. It was nice and quiet after that.'

Russo turned to Blanchard. 'I don't know if that has anything to do with your missing rancher, Sheriff, but it sounded like something I thought you should know about.'

Blanchard looked down at Barnwell and nodded. 'Yeah, I guess it all helps. Can you describe the man you say stomped out of the saloon?'

'Yeah. He was a young, soft-looking man. Tall and wasn't wearing any hat that I saw. Had a lot of red hair. Red on the head like a dick on a dog, my pappy would have said. I didn't see where he went.'

The sheriff looked at Matt and frowned. 'Had to be the Neely boy.' He turned to Russo and shook his head. 'Thanks for letting me hear this. Come on, Kendrick. I guess my dirty work isn't over yet.' The lawman waved at the two men, and he and Matt turned back out to the street.

'Damn fool kid,' Blanchard said. 'I didn't think he'd do something stupid like that.'

Matt agreed. 'He sounded like a hothead, but not a fool.'

'Ah, he's a good kid, all right. Been under his pa's thumb all his life. His mother died when he was a young'un and I expect it hasn't been easy with a strict-minded man like the reverend. Now, I gotta go arrest him. This hasn't been my day; first having to tell that young girl about her father and now going to arrest Jonathan. It just hasn't been my day.'

Matt begged off helping with taking the Neely boy into custody, and left the sheriff at the hotel. A short time later, sitting in the restaurant with another pot of coffee, he listened to others talk about the arrest of the preacher's son. The story about finding the cattleman's body in the river was the main topic and everybody seemed to have their own idea of what it meant. Most, it seemed, were starting to think like the preacher, that the town was turning into a kind of hell.

CHAPTER 8

Susan Harcourt was apparently holding up as well as could be expected. Accompanied by Claire Blanchard, she had gone to the undertaker's to say goodbye to her only parent. Later, from his chair on the hotel porch, Matt had watched the comings and goings of the town. For a few minutes he watched a very nondescript black-and-white dog making its way on the other side of the dirt street. The dog's nose was close to the ground as he smelled his way along the edge of the sidewalk. Probably searching for a tomcat to attack, Matt thought. No small town seemed complete without its population of stray dogs and cats.

The mongrel was careful to keep away from any of the horses tied to the rails in front of the town's businesses. For a community this size, there seemed to be a lot of traffic. With the arrival of cattlemen and buyers, business was brisk at the hotel, the restaurant next door and the town's only saloon down at the end of the block. From their clothes it was easy to make out those men who were here to conduct cattle business. Nearly all the cattle buyers arrived from the East by train and were dressed in suits and flat-heeled shoes. Round, hard derby hats set them apart from the ranchers, who favored wide-brimmed Stetsons. The ranchers, except for Harcourt and his friend Joad Howard, had ridden in from their nearby cattle spreads. The two Californians had enjoyed one of the first rides over the Sierras on the recently completed rail connection.

With regular traffic yet to be scheduled, the trip had been a historic event.

Without looking at his pocket watch, Matt knew it had to be getting close to lunch; his stomach was letting him know. His thoughts about a meal were interrupted when he heard loud yelling coming from down the street. Curious, he left the porch and strolled down the sidewalk toward the sheriff's office.

'Sheriff, you can't lock my son up. Not for something he didn't do.' The preacher, Reverend Neely was standing in the sheriff's doorway, yelling in his deep voice. 'My son may have taken up the argument against turning this town into a place of ill repute, but he would never break one of the commandments. He wouldn't hurt anyone,' finished the preacher. His voice dropped and his last words were more of a plea than a demand.

'Reverend, I gotta agree. I don't think Jonathan did kill that man. Apparently he drank more than was good for him and got drunk. I found him passed out in one of the horse stalls in the stable. But he was heard telling others that he knew how to take care of things. And as he's not been able to account for where he was the rest of the night, well, I just have to lock him up.'

Sheriff Blanchard stood in his office doorway. 'Now, you can go in and talk with the boy if you want, but I can't let you in the cell with him; you'll have to talk through the bars.'

With his shoulders slumped, the tall thin man nodded. Head hanging, he walked past the lawman.

'Excuse me.' Susan Harcourt brushed past Matt and entered the sheriff's office. 'Sheriff. Someone has broken into our hotel rooms,' she said, her voice trembling. 'They've been turned upside down.'

CHAPTER 9

Matt was getting used to following along behind the sheriff, and the sheriff didn't seem to mind. The lawman only nodded when entering the girl's room. Kendrick was right behind him. Susan, with a woman whom Matt took to be the sheriff's wife standing beside her, had remained in the hallway.

The girl had been right. The mattress was in tatters and clothes were strewn in piles on the floor. All the drawers in the single desk had been pulled out and turned over. Even the few dresses left hanging in the curtained-off wardrobe had been thrown aside. The sheriff strode to the door connecting her room with her father's, from where he could see even more destruction.

Looking over his shoulder, Matt saw the damage. The mattress, like that in Susan's room had been slashed and even the sides of the dead man's valise had been cut. Boots and shirts were tossed around the floor and the drawers of a small writing desk had been pulled out and left in a pile on the bed.

'Miz Harcourt,' Sheriff Blanchard said, standing in the middle of the room with his hands on his hips. 'Can you tell what has been stolen?'

For a moment the young woman simply looked at Blanchard, Matt supposed that she was wondering what the sheriff meant. 'I can't really say, Sheriff. I mean, there wasn't much for anyone to steal. Father wasn't carrying any money. He

38

only brought enough for this trip. I can't think of anything he'd have that would be of value to anyone.'

'How about your things? Is there anything missing?'

For a moment all the young woman could do was to look blankly around the room. 'Not that I can tell,' she said, shaking her head. 'A few pieces of jewelry, a couple necklaces and a silver bracelet were in one of the drawers.' Matt watched as her hand went to a thin gold chain she wore around her neck, disappearing into the bodice of her dress. 'I came to pack up my things. I opened the door and found it like this. I don't know why someone would think there was anything worth stealing in here.'

Sheriff Blanchard stood for a moment longer, then shrugged. 'I don't see anything that'll tell me who could have done this. Probably just some lowlife thinking that with nobody here, he'd take a look. I'm terribly sorry. What with everything that's happening to you, I expect you'll be wanting to take your pa's body back over the mountains.'

'No, Sheriff,' she said defiantly. 'I won't leave until the business Father was here for is taken care of. Your wife has kindly invited me to stay at your house until I can finish with the cattle business. There is no other family back at the ranch, so I've decided he can be buried here. We don't even have a burial ground on the property and the nearest town is half a day's ride away. One place is as good as another.'

'Well, you're certainly welcome to stay with us. But in any case, I doubt whether we'll find out who did this.'

'It doesn't look like my clothes were damaged and if all that's missing is my jewelry, then it isn't so bad.'

'I'll tell everyone in town to keep a lookout for anyone trying to sell your bracelet or necklaces, but I wouldn't expect too much.'

Feeling helpless, the two men could only stand by and watch as Susan and the sheriff's wife started cleaning up the mess, picking up the clothes and carefully folding each piece. After a few moments Matt decided he was not needed and, with a pat on the back of the lawman, left.

His stomach was still growling for attention, so he headed next door for the restaurant. He took his time over a final cup of coffee while he sat and thought about all that had happened since his arrival. There was little reason to believe the murder of the California rancher or the break in of the dead man's room had anything to do with the gold-shipping information. It had been a California business man he was to meet, not an old rancher. That whole affair could be because someone had the notion that the cattleman was carrying valuables. But, thinking back to the knife attack on the train, it occurred to Matt that someone could want to make sure the Californian was actually a rancher and not the messenger. That would explain his rooms being gone through.

Thinking about it didn't help the former Army officer out, though. He didn't know whom he was to meet or how whoever it would be would know who he was. Disgusted with the whole thing, he paid for his meal and walked across to the saloon. It might be early in the day, but the thought of topping off his meal with a cold beer sounded good.

After letting his eyes adjust from the bright sunlight outside to the dimness in the long room, Matt stepped up to the long bar and ordered the beer. He took a sip of the brew and relaxed, leaning one elbow on the wood and a foot on the brass rail. Looking over the long room, he saw only a few customers. Half a dozen or so tables took up most of the space, each with a number of chairs. Only a couple of the tables had early-afternoon drinkers sitting at them. At one table far in the back three men hunched over the felt tabletop, playing a quiet game of poker.

'The rumors say that Clarence was killed for his wallet.' Matt hadn't noticed the man now standing beside him. He turned and he saw a tall, older man leaning against the bar. He wondered if this was the businessman he was waiting to meet up with.

40

'I seen you with the sheriff. My name's Joad Howard, I'm Clarence Harcourt's best friend. Or I was, anyway. I wonder if I can talk with you a bit?'

'Sure. But there isn't much I can tell you that you probably don't already know,' said Matt, shaking the offered hand. Taking a closer look, he saw that Howard's face didn't have the tired look his slumped shoulders suggested. The man's thick eyebrows shaded his eyes, though, giving him a guarded look. 'I don't know if the sheriff has laid your friend's murder on robbery, though.'

Signaling to the bartender for a beer, Howard slowly shook his head. 'I'd hate to think he was killed because he was a cattleman. They've got someone in jail, but nobody seems to think he really had anything to do with Clarence's death.'

'I know. There was a lot of yelling earlier, and the young man was one of the loudest talking against having you cattlemen here. But somehow I agree. That fellow didn't strike me as being a killer.'

'There are some strong feelings about the idea of this becoming a shipping point for ranchers in this part of the country,' Howard said. 'You know, there're a lot of cattle over in the San Joaquin Valley. For a long time we've been able to sell our beef to the miners. Some of our cattle was put on river steamers and sent down to the wharves in San Francisco even, and put on ships, but that market didn't make a hill of beans. It's the railroad that'll make the difference. Getting our stock to the markets in the East will make some ranchers a lot of money.'

CHAPTER 10

For a time neither man spoke, each thinking his own thoughts. 'I imagine you fought in the Great War? You've got the look of a military man.' Howard asked.

'Yes, and I saw more than enough,' Matt answered; wondering again if this was the man he was waiting for. Wasn't being a cattleman considered being a businessman? He decided to wait to see if the California rancher would slip him an envelope. 'When it was all over, I decided to come on out West to see what the part of the country that hadn't been fought over looked like.'

Howard smiled and didn't come up with any paper of any kind. 'Fortunately I was already out here when that all started. Clarence and I came out when gold was first discovered back in '49. It didn't take a genius to see that standing knee-deep in the river, bent over washing gravel all day would be a good way to make a living. Yeah, a lot of men did get rich that way,' he added quickly, 'but that kind of work wasn't what we wanted to do.'

Matt sipped his beer and didn't say anything. Obviously the man wanted to talk.

'We had left Nebraska Territory that year, just in time to get through the Sierra Mountains before winter closed the passes. When we got to the gold country, all we could see were men standing in the freezing water trying to pan out a living. We decided that wasn't for us.' The older man stood, leaning

42

against the wood, eyes staring unseeing at the bar.

While listening to the man Matt had let his own eyes wander over the array of dusty bottles, few with labels he recognized. Most were whiskeys but here and there was one with some kind of clear liquor inside. Probably gin, he thought, or maybe even some of that alcohol made from potatoes. During the war there had been a man in his company who, given a few days' rest, would find a way of making a clear waterlike liquor. It seemed that all he needed was a sack of potatoes, which he probably stole, and a tub or barrel. What else it took Matt never knew but in only a couple days he'd find a small bottle of the drink in his tent. As company captain, Matt figured the bottle was payment for not asking questions.

'Old Clarence was a smart one, he was. I'll miss him,' Howard said after a while. 'It was his idea not to go searching for a claim. Someone, he said, would have to provide meat for those working the goldfields. Well, we knew how to do that a lot better than we knew about finding nuggets. It was his idea to supply beef to the diggings. He'd heard about some Spaniards down at El Pueblo de Los Angeles. We brought back half a dozen head that we'd paid next to nothing for and as fast as you could say beef we had them butchered and sold. The next trip we had to pay more for the cattle; those Spaniards were pretty quick to catch on. But that time we brought back a mixed lot, bulls, heifers and some young stuff. That was the start of both our ranches.'

Matt, taken up by the story, smiled. 'I reckon you two made your fortune a lot easier than most of those men who were after gold.'

'Yeah. We had to fight for it though, once in a while, when one or another of those miners decided our cattle were wild and free for the taking. But all in all, we did pretty good. Enough,' he said, turning to look at Matt, 'that we sent for our families. I had a wife and two sons back in Nebraska and Clarence had his wife and daughter. They all came out together.'

43

'Young Susan Harcourt must have been real young.'

'She was a mite younger than my boys. That was, what, about twelve or thirteen years ago. My boys are just turned twenty-four and twenty-five now. She's about twenty or twenty-one, I'd say.'

'So you two have been building your ranches for almost twelve years?'

'A little more, I guess. They've been good years, too. Of course, there were a few bad years and we took our losses. My Colleen died of cholera when the boys were just getting into long pants. Clarence's wife was killed coming across. Indians attacked the wagon train. The wagon master told us he thought the redskins were more than likely after whiskey. They killed four or five people, then gave up and rode away. Susan's mother was one of those killed.' Again, lost in his memories, the old man stared off into space.

'There's one thing that can be said about Susan Harcourt,' Howard went on after a time. 'She's got what it takes. She gets it naturally. The wagon master told me that Susan had been helping her ma, loading one rifle as her ma helped fight off the crazy Indians.' He turned to make sure the younger man understood the importance of what he was being told and smiled, his head high as if proud of the girl. 'When her ma was hit, she didn't stop but took the loaded rifle and started shooting at the attackers. That old wagon master said he didn't doubt that she hit a few of them, too.'

Neither man said anything for a while, resting both elbows to the bar, letting the mahogany take their weight as they relaxed, thinking about what such a battle would do to most young girls.

Eventually, finishing his glass of beer, Matt came to the conclusion that this was not the man he was waiting for. He was just thinking that he'd go back out into the sunshine when he stopped as Howard shook himself and motioned for the bartender to bring two more glasses.

'It was because of the Great War that Clarence and I decided

44

to make the trip over here on the train,' he said, once more looking at Matt.

Ah, maybe he was carrying the envelope after all. 'That war's been over for a while now,' Kendrick offered, accepting both the beer and the continuation of the older man's company.

'Yep. We read that the Eastern market was crying for beef, so Clarence and I figured we'd see about sending a herd to that market. Maybe, we thought, we could make some profit from our cattle and help take a little pressure off the new president.'

Neither man had been paying any attention to the men around them in the saloon. The first they knew they weren't alone was when they heard harsh laughter. Standing a few feet behind them was Ivan Russo and his foreman.

'Now isn't that just like a Yankee sympathizer?' Russo laughed. 'Ready to do whatever it takes to help out their cause, as long as it makes them money.' The rancher cuffed his Stetson back on his head, bellied up to the bar and called out to the bartender,

'Bring these two another beer. Even if they are Yankees, old Grogan here and I will buy them a drink.' The foreman, not letting any expression show on his long face, took a place on the other side of his boss. The faint sound of bells could be heard when the man moved. Matt figured it was the sound of the silver conchos on his pants legs hitting each other.

'I take it you are backers of the South?' Howard asked, pushing the new glass of beer away and picking up his half-drunk schooner.

'Well, being this far from the battles, all we could do was cheer them Southern boys on,' Russo said, not paying any attention to the gesture. 'Seems to me, though, some bad decisions were made by both sides. The Southern states could hardly expect to match the wherewithal of the northern states. However, from what was in the newspapers, I do believe that those secessionists could fight a better fight than the Yankees. All things being equal, which they were not, the outcome could have been very different.'

Matt listened, first watching Russo's face and then glancing at Grogan. Somehow the foreman's deadpan impassiveness bothered him.

'Well,' he said in the silence that followed Russo's comments, 'it doesn't matter much any more. The war is over and the country is working at getting things back together. Whether anyone wore the blue and gold or a butternut uniform, those days are past. And it's a damn good thing, too. From what I saw, that war was not a good thing for anyone on either side.'

'You were in it?' Russo asked. 'Having a ranching operation to run, I missed out. Pa wouldn't hear of my going East to join up and by the time he died, well, it was all over. I wanted to, though. You never know,' he said, smiling at Matt. 'If it had gone on a bit longer we might have met on a battlefield somewhere. You in your blue and gold, and me scaring the hell out everybody with my bloodcurdling Rebel yell.' He turned to Grogan and laughed.

'You've been reading too many of those dime novels, Russo,' said Matt. 'The "bloodcurdling Rebel yell" was more a bit of some writer's imagination than anything. I don't recall, after the first couple of major battles, ever hearing it. But, as I said a minute ago, that's all over now.' Finishing his beer, Matt nodded to the rancher. 'Thanks for the beer, but I reckon I've had enough for this afternoon. Maybe next time I'll buy you one.' He tipped his hat toward the men and walked toward the door.

'Yeah,' he heard Howard say before following him out on to the sidewalk and into the sunshine.

'There is something about that man I just don't like,' Howard man said as the two men stood on the sidewalk and took in the town.

'Ah, I reckon he's just not got his full growth yet. It's that foreman of his that I wonder about,' said Kendrick. 'That man just doesn't seem to smile. Can't trust a man who doesn't smile.'

CHAPTER 11

Thinking he'd give whoever he was waiting for every opportunity to approach him, Matt decided to relax in one of the chairs on the hotel porch. His sitting there, out in the open, would make it easy for the person with the message for which he'd come to Hunter's Crossing to pass it on. That was the idea, anyhow. So far no one he'd met had given any indication that such a thing would happen.

From his vantage point he was able to witness the comings and goings of the town, though. After Joad Howard had left him, saying something about beer in the afternoon making him sleepy, Matt had taken up his place on the porch. A short time later he watched as Russo left the saloon and, striding with a swagger, like he owned the world, went down the street to the town stable. There was no sign of Russo's dour foreman. Within minutes, the Nevada rancher came out on the back of a beautiful black horse. The saddle the man sat on sparkled with silver trim.

'A real fancy dude,' Matt Kendrick said to himself. 'Both rancher and foreman.' Russo nodded as he rode by and Matt watched as he rode down the street and across the bridge. 'Wonder where his foreman and that hired hand of his got to?' he mused.

For a time, the sun-filled main street seemed to doze under the early evening sun. The only movement was a black-and-white dog, making its way up the street, stopping at every post

47

and beam to smell who'd been there before. Matt himself had almost drifted off but was brought abruptly awake by the sound of a door slamming in the distance.

Quickly scanning the length of the street, he saw that nothing had changed. The dog was a little farther along in his inspection, and had reached the sheriff's office when the office door was roughly pushed open, sending the animal out of sight under the sidewalk. Matt watched as the young red-headed man came out, followed by his father and Sheriff Blanchard. For a moment the three stood talking before father and son turned and walked up the street, coming toward the hotel.

Matt heard the hotel door swing open behind him. He turned in his chair to see Susan Harcourt and the sheriff's wife coming through. Both women were carrying pieces of the younger woman's luggage. The difference in the two women was more than that one was a few years older. Being married gave Claire Blanchard a more settled look, Matt thought, but then decided he couldn't really explain what he meant.

The two were about the same height and both, it looked to him, were about the same dress size. Claire's hair was dark brown and didn't have the sparkle that the Harcourt girl's black hair had. For all that, her brown hair hung down her back in soft waves and bounced in rhythm with her stride. Neither woman was smiling as the pair came out on to the hotel porch.

'Here,' Matt said, jumping up, 'let me help you ladies with those.'

Susan Harcourt smiled and had started to say something when she looked past him. 'Oh!' She made a sound and, letting her smile fade, dropped the carpetbag she had been carrying. Matt glanced around and saw that she had seen the man accused of killing her father.

Caleb and Jonathan Neely had been walking up the street, engaged in a heated discussion, oblivious to everything. Hearing Susan's soft cry, Jonathan looked up at the young woman standing on the sidewalk. Instantly he pulled his arm from his father's grasp and stopped.

'Miss Harcourt,' he said pleadingly, 'I did not have anything to do with your father's death. Believe me.'

Susan Harcourt, her face pale, made no reply but stood slowly shaking her head.

Not taking his eyes off the young woman, the young man grimaced. He knew the image he presented was not positive. What the grieving woman saw before her was a drunk who had spent the night in jail, his clothes dirty and torn, and his hair matted and uncombed. He shook his head and quickly turned away.

'Here,' Matt said again. He reached to take the heavy suitcase from Claire Blanchard's hand, picked up the bag that Susan Harcourt had dropped, and started walking in the other direction. 'Let me carry those for you.'

Kendrick let the sheriff take one of the pieces of baggage and the two men fell in behind as the women headed toward the Blanchard home.

Once there the two men left the women to settle in and walked back toward the main street. Matt asked about the Neely boy being released from jail.

'I had to let him go,' Sheriff Blanchard said. 'He couldn't have had anything to do with the break-in at Harcourt's rooms, and as for his story of being drunk and not remembering where he had been the night the cattleman had been killed, well, I don't think that's enough to keep him locked up. He won't go anywhere and the circuit judge will be in town in a week or so. Yeah, I let him out.'

'I don't know him or his father, but it seems more likely that it was the preacher, not the son who was angry enough to do murder,' was Matt's comment. 'Come on, I'll buy you a cup of coffee.'

Before the two could enter the restaurant, they were stopped by a call from across the street.

'Sheriff,' the thin hotel clerk yelled from the hotel porch.

'You better come quick, there's been another killing.'

The sheriff rushed across to get the news. 'It's that rancher up on the second floor. Howard. His head's been bashed in.'

CHAPTER 12

Once again Matt followed right behind Blanchard as the lawman sped up the hotel stairs. Men, standing around the open door to a room, stood quickly aside as the two men shouldered them out of the way.

The room, smaller than either of the rooms the Harcourts had taken, was a mess. The mattress had been cut open and tufts of straw and cotton batting torn out. Broken pieces of the enameled water bowl and basin were scattered across the floor and the doors of the wardrobe had been wrenched open. One door hung from a single hinge while the other was leaning against a wall. Even the curtain over the single window had been ripped off and was on the floor.

Lying on a pile of shirts and pants, Howard's body was curled up and looked somehow shriveled and old. Matt could see bits of white bone showing through the bloody mess that had been the back of his head. Both arms were bent at the elbows, his forearms covering the front of his head protectively.

'Just like Harcourt's rooms,' Blanchard said unnecessarily. 'Impossible to tell if whoever did this found what he was looking for, but I'll bet he didn't. Maybe someone thought these ranchers were carrying money. I don't know, but my guess is the same person did this as killed Harcourt.'

'If that's true, Sheriff,' Reverend Neely pushed his way into the room, 'then you can stop hounding my son. He has been

51

home, cleaning himself up and washing his clothes since you let him out of jail.'

'Reverend, you always seem to get into the middle of things, don't you? Have you given any thought to the idea that clobbering these two ranchers could be the work of some of your "good" town's people?' It was obvious to Matt that the sheriff was losing his temper. 'You've been preaching the suggestion that if the ranchers and the cattle buyers go away this town will go on being a God-fearing place. Now, it could be said that some one of your flock has decided that this is a way to discourage the cattle business from staying here. Has that crossed your mind?'

Neely drew himself up straight and, looking around to make sure he had an audience, let go. 'Sheriff, it is obvious that you don't have any notion who is responsible. Stop throwing out accusations and start doing your job. I suggest you find out where each of the other cattlemen was when this poor man was killed. There is where you'll find your mad killer, Sheriff.'

Sheriff Blanchard, calming down a little, simply shook his head. 'No, I don't follow that, Reverend. But I will ask those questions. And not just of the cattlemen and buyers; also of a few of your righteous town people.'

'I know it isn't charitable to say this,' the Reverend Neely said, himself relaxing his anger, 'but if these cattle people keep killing each other, this town may not end up becoming the Sodom and Gomorrah that we good people fear it will.'

Again, Sheriff Blanchard's face grew hard. 'What exactly do you mean, Reverend, "these cattle people killing each other". Are you claiming that other ranchers caused the two deaths? Or are you just pointing the finger at the cattle buyers, hoping that's the case? Either way, I don't see how that would make any sense.'

'Oh, no, Sheriff. I wouldn't dream of accusing anyone. It's just that before all these men came to town we hadn't had any murders and now we've had two. Why, I can't recall the last time there was even a theft reported here in Hunter's Crossing, and all you have to do is look at the rooms these folks were staying in to know thieves have been at work. How can anyone with even a little intelligence not conclude that your allowing these cattlemen and the buyers to come in and take over our town is not tied in?'

Blanchard's voice was harsh. 'Reverend Neely, as I've said before, neither you nor I can stop the railroad's plans. The shipping pens are on railroad property and can't be legally stopped. How they run their business is not up to you and there's certainly nothing I can do about it. I would be careful with your accusations.'

'But Sheriff, I am not accusing anyone. It was my son who was falsely accused, you will remember. Yes, I admit, he did let the evil of whiskey blind his thinking, but it is equally clear that he could not have committed murder.'

'The circuit judge will have to decide that, when he arrives. Meanwhile, I will keep asking if anyone knows anything that can help me.'

'And I keep saying, Sheriff, let the cattle people kill themselves. It isn't Christian, but it is vital that we keep our town clean and righteous.'

Having had enough, Sheriff Blanchard was silent for a moment and then told everyone to leave the room. 'Maybe I can find something that'll point in a direction. Meanwhile, you all clear out. Go about your business.'

After asking someone to notify the undertaker Blanchard shut the door and turned to Matt. 'Well, once again, we get to see what we can see. I certainly hope that the perpetrator isn't one of those men who are in favor of this idea of shipping cattle the railroad is proposing. Hell, I'll be happy if we can ever find out who's got it in for these two ranchers.'

Blanchard turned the dead man over and saw that the man's shirt tail had come out of the top of his pants. Under the shirt and tight against his stomach was the brown canvas of a money belt.

'I reckon the killer didn't find this,' he said, pulling it free. He righted the small table that had once carried the water pitcher and bowl, laid the belt down and opened the pockets.

Matt, thinking about the message Colonel Cummings wanted him to get, paid close attention. He hid his disappointment when the sheriff found only a few gold coins and a thin sheaf of bills. He counted the money and looked at Matt.

'Well, if he was killed for his money, the killer missed out on the grand total of just under a hundred dollars. Not very much when it's your life, is it?'

'I just can't believe someone would take the risk of doing this,' Matt said, speaking for the first time, 'for that little dab of money. Especially if he came up empty-handed. I'm not a Pinkerton detective, Sheriff, but I have to think there is something else going on here.'

CHAPTER 13

Most of those standing solemnly in the town's cemetery the next morning were obviously ranchers and cattle buyers. The few locals stood off to one side of the newly dug grave. Reverend Neely had not been asked to officiate at the burial of Clarence Harcourt. Susan had told Sheriff Blanchard she wanted to keep it simple and asked if he would like to say a few words.

'I didn't get to know this man very well,' the sheriff started off, holding his hat with both hands and looking down into the deep darkness. 'He came to our town peacefully to conduct legal business and someone killed him. While I can't talk about him, I can assure everyone that this is, for the most part, a good town. Mr Harcourt found it so. We had a talk about what the railroad would mean to both the town and to California cattle-men. He was a man who thought positively. He had been through the gold rush and had learned that only with hard work, whether digging for the yellow metal, raising stock or as a shop owner was it possible to have true success. So I can add that he was that: a hard worker.

'I've gotten to know his daughter, Susan. She is what we would all want our daughters to be, bright, intelligent and full of life. That tells us more about her father. He set the example that she followed. So, while I don't know much about this man we are sending off this morning, I can tell you I've learned he was a good man. One who might have made a difference, a positive difference in our town. But he wasn't given the chance, was he?'

With only a few tears coursing down her cheeks, Susan Harcourt stepped to the edge of the grave and, not saying anything, dropped the bunch of flowers she had been holding on to the pineboard casket. She and Claire Blanchard had walked together up the hill from town and now, arm in arm, they made their way back.

In groups of two or three, those attending the brief ceremony followed. Other than giving the sheriff a nod as they passed out of the fenced limits of the cemetery the mourners were silent. Matt Kendrick had stood to one side and was one of the last to leave.

Cemeteries, he thought, whether near one of the battlefields or here on a windswept hillside were, for some reason, places where only birds and a scampering squirrel or two seemed comfortable. Standing alone, he looked over the town below. Two men were dead and for no reason that either he nor the sheriff could determine. I certainly hope this has nothing to do with the information the colonel sent me out to get, he thought.

As they walked down the track to town, he asked the sheriff if he was ready for a cup of coffee.

'Now that sounds good, Mr Kendrick – anything that'll get my mind off everything that's happened recently. But,' Blanchard paused to look down the street, 'somehow I think that group of men over by my office are waiting to talk to me. I'd better hear them out. I don't know any of them, so it's likely they are either stockmen or buyers and I doubt they have anything good to tell me.'

The five or six men standing on the plank sidewalk waited patiently as the two men approached. The sheriff glanced at them as they stood aside to let the lawman through, opened the office door and motioned them to come in. He went behind his scarred desk and sat down. Matt waited, followed the last of the men in, and found a place against a wall to lean against.

'Gentlemen, this hasn't been a morning the town can take pride in. I imagine you're here to talk about what's been happening?'

One of the men stepped forward a bit and nodded. 'Sheriff, I'm Silas Pepper. My spread is on down the river. Me and the boys here are a mite worried. We came here at the railroad's invitation to talk about shipping our beef East. There's been two cattlemen killed since we came to town and the railroad people aren't here yet to talk to us.' Pepper paused for a minute and looked around at the others as if to make sure he had their support. 'Now some of us don't have a need for this,' he went on. 'For sometime most of us have been shipping our beef from over at the railhead at Carson City. We don't need to bring them this way, to Hunter's Crossing. It's a longer drive over to Carson City for the most of us but maybe it's worth it if coming here means getting killed.'

Sheriff Blanchard nodded his agreement. 'Yeah, this hasn't worked out like the railroad folks said it would. But you can't blame the people of Hunter's Crossing for either of those murders.'

'Oh yeah?' one of the other ranchers said, anger thickening his voice. 'Seems you had someone in your jail after that California fella was killed. Only you let him go and now there's another one dead.'

'Wait just a minute there,' Blanchard said loudly. 'I let the Neely boy go because he couldn't have had anything to do with Harcourt's death. And as for Howard's murder, I haven't had any time to even start looking into that. It looks to have happened this morning and, well, there was a funeral to go to, wasn't there?'

Sheriff Blanchard let his eyes drop to the scuffed top of his desk. Along with the badge, the desk and other furniture had been part of what he had inherited when taking the job after Sheriff Hunter had died. Hunter had had a habit of putting his boots up on the desk. He also had a bad habit of wearing short blunt spurs, which he never removed from his boot heels. Blunt they might have been, but they had made their mark on the desktop.

'Boys, I don't know what I can do.' He looked up and let his eyes range around the room, catching the gaze of each man in turn. 'All I can say is that I'm doing what I can. Actually, I've asked for the help of Mr Matt Kendrick, back there,' he said, pointing to the back of the room. 'Kendrick is a former Army officer and has some experience in such things. He's not a Pinkerton man, mind you, but he has some military training. All we can ask is that you don't panic. Let us do our job.'

Matt stood a little straighter as each of the ranchers gave him the once over. Not sure what Blanchard was doing, he tried to keep his poker face on, not to let his dismay show.

'Now,' Sheriff Blanchard continued, 'if you will excuse us, we've got a lot of things to do. And we will be looking into everything that has been happening here in town.'

'OK, Sheriff, but some of us don't see much reason to hang around much longer. We all got work to do.'

Blanchard nodded. 'That part of things is between you and the railroad. It would be good for the town if this becomes a shipping point and I know the railroad wants it so that those stock ranches over on the other side of the mountains can ship East. I would expect the railroad to be real interested in what's been happening, but I can't speak for them.'

Not showing whether they agreed or not, the ranchers filed out, each one giving Matt another brief inspection. When the door closed and only the two of them were left in the room, Matt looked at the sheriff.

'What the hell are you getting me into, telling those men that I was helping you?'

'I had to tell them something and there you were, leaning against the wall. Anyway, you've been hanging around, in my back pocket every time I looked up. You got to admit, you've stuck close since coming into town. I figure you've got something going on that you're not telling me, so . . . well . . . I had to tell them something,' Blanchard finished lamely.

Matt held the lawman's eyes for a minute, thinking. 'I don't have any such experience that'll help you get answers. Why'd you have to lie to them and tell them I did? They're going to expect results now.'

'They will expect results anyhow. And I didn't tell them you had law experience. If you listened, I told them you were not a Pinkerton detective, but you had army experience. I didn't lie to them. You did say you were in the army, didn't you?'

Shaking his head, Matt snorted. 'That sounds like a lawyer talking, not exactly lying but skirting around the truth.'

Blanchard laughed. 'That's probably because I am a lawyer. I only took this badge because I thought it'd help me get to know the town before I opened my law office. If I decide to run for county judge it'll look good to the voters if I have worn the badge for a while.' He stood up and held out his hand. 'Come on. I can use the help and you've been right alongside me anyway.'

Slowly, not sure what he was getting into, Matt took the hand and shook it once.

'OK, but that means you have to pay for the coffee.' He smiled and then added, 'boss.'

CHAPTER 14

Claire Oglby had met Morgan Blanchard when he arrived in Cheyenne. Her father was the county judge and she served as his secretary, keeping records and filing all the paperwork his office seemed to generate. Judge Oglby had had his office in the courthouse since she was a little girl and during the years when her mother had sat at the desk outside the judge's chambers, Claire had played on the floor, near by. It seemed only natural that when she was old enough and had gone through Mrs Thompson's School for Young Women she would take her mother's place in the office.

For a while that had been exciting for the young woman, meeting all the people who came in to see the judge. Even having such an important man for a father had made her proud, but when men like the mayor or some government official entered the office it was heady stuff.

But even that paled when, one morning with the sun shining through the second-floor windows, a young man opened the office door and walked in. Looking up, Claire was instantly glad she'd worn her best dress to work that morning. Unconsciously patting her hair as he came to stand before her desk, she smiled and waited for him to speak.

Life in the office took on new meaning for her when Morgan Blanchard, just graduated from law school, became law clerk to the judge. It took almost three months before he seemed to take notice of her and then only because he'd been invited to dinner at the Oglbys. Later he swore that that wasn't true.

'I saw you the moment I opened your father's door,' he told her when it came up later, 'but you were just too beautiful for me to think you'd take notice of me.'

Their courtship lasted another six months. Married in a big church wedding with many of those important friends of her father's attending, the newly married couple set up house-keeping in a newly purchased house. Life for the Blanchards was full and happy until one morning, Claire was told of her parents' deaths.

The train on which the Oglbys had been returning from a meeting in Prescott, Arizona, had been derailed; the engine and first three cars had come off the tracks. More than a dozen passengers in those cars were killed, the Oglbys among them.

Finding it hard to be anywhere near what had been her father's offices, Claire left work. But staying home all day while her husband was in the court chambers started wearing on her. Eventually, seeing how unhappy his wife was becoming, Morgan resigned and, after being married only two years, the newlyweds headed West. Soon after arriving in Hunter's Crossing, Morgan had accepted the sheriff's job, a position Claire Blanchard thought was a waste of her husband's legal skills. Now, with two murders happening, she was starting to get worried about the safety of such a job.

Claire Blanchard and Susan Harcourt had gone straight back to the Blanchards' house after the funeral. Sitting silently at the cloth-covered kitchen table, their thoughts were still on the morning's event. Bone white porcelain cups, decorated with colorful flowers, sat ready for the tea water to boil.

'What will you do now, Susan?' Only a few years older than her guest, it seemed to Claire that she was now talking to a much younger girl.

'I'll stay and meet with the railroad officials, just as Father was to do,' Susan answered. 'No matter what has happened, there is still the ranch, and being able to ship our stock will make a big difference.'

'But . . . well, do you think those railroad officials will accept you taking your father's place?'

'It doesn't matter whether they do or not,' the younger woman said. 'All they should be interested in is whether we can ship the cattle we say we can. Claire, you have no idea how many head there are on ranches on that side of the mountains. Father was here to find out what the costs would be and when the rail link would be scheduled. I can take that information back to the ranchers.'

'You are a strong woman,' the sheriff's wife said, pouring the steeped tea. 'I don't think I have ever been what anyone would call strong. At least, not like that.'

'You never know what you can do until you have to do it. That's what my father always told me. "Stay calm and do what you think is right", he'd say. Staying calm and thinking before acting was his way.'

A knock on the front door interrupted the two young women. Going to the door, Claire opened it to find a well-dressed stranger standing on the porch.

'Mrs Blanchard? My name is Ivan Russo. Is Miss Harcourt available? I realize this is likely a bad time, but I wanted to extend my condolences.'

Russo stood tall and straight, his black wool pants well-brushed and tucked into the tops of recently blackened high heeled boots. The white shirt he wore was almost covered by the black silk vest, both mostly hidden by his long-skirted riding-coat.

'Why, let me see if she is seeing anyone,' Claire said. She closed the door softly, leaving the young man on the porch, and hurried back to the kitchen.

'Susan, if I didn't know better, I'd think you have a suitor.

There's a young man on the porch wanting to extend his condolences. Mr Russo, I think he said his name is.'

'I really don't . . .' Susan started to say, then stopped. 'Oh, I suppose I had better see him. I don't feel like it, but I had better.'

She went to the door, opened it and faced the man. Not having been sure what to expect, she was surprised to find herself looking up at a man whose smile spread from ear to ear.

'Miss Harcourt.' His voice was soft while at the same time firm. 'I don't want to bother you, especially today. But I would like to tell you how sorry I am. If there is anything I can do to help you, please don't hesitate to call on me.'

Susan let a small smile cross her face. 'Thank you, Mister – oh, I'm afraid Claire didn't tell me your name.'

'Ivan Russo,' he said offering his hand. 'I have a small spread a little north of here.'

She shook his hand and looked into his eyes. 'Well, Mr Russo, thank you for your sympathy and your offer. Losing my father has not been easy and especially here, so far from the home ranch.'

'I can only imagine,' Russo said, still holding her hand and not seeming bothered by her direct look. 'However, if I can help with anything, from talking to the railroad people when they get here or helping you get back to your side of the mountains, well, I only want to help.'

Gently pulling her hand free, she repeated herself. 'I thank you, but I'll be all right when the officials get here. I have my fare ready and hope to get this all taken care of in the next couple days. There is a big celebration in Monterey late next week: the inauguration of the new governor. My father was one of his main supporters and, well, I'd like to be there to represent our family.'

'Well, if there is anything, just let me know,' Russo said. He tipped his hat and moved down the steps. With a wave he pushed through the gate of the picket fence and walked down the street toward the main business section of town.

'Now, that was nice of him, don't you think, Susan?' Claire asked, peeking through the curtain of a front window. 'He is an attractive man.'

'I guess so. However, I have too much to do now to be thinking about men, attractive or not.'

Claire, a small smile flitting across her face, nodded her silent agreement.

CHAPTER 15

As it was getting along toward noon, Sheriff Blanchard suggested they take an early lunch with their coffee.

'It'll give us a chance to talk,' he said, leading the way across to the restaurant. The black-and-white mongrel that Matt had seen before on the street was ambling along near the plank sidewalk, nose to the ground as if smelling the trail to a dog treasure.

'Anybody belong to that dog?' he asked as the two men stepped up on to the sidewalk.

'Not that I ever saw. It's just the town dog, I guess. Someone must feed it and it must have a place to sleep, but I've never seen it anywhere or doing anything but that, scouring the streets.'

After ordering their meal, they sipped coffee as the food was being prepared and talked about the two killings. Throughout the meal – fried ham slices, mashed potatoes and gravy and canned peas that had been heated in butter with pieces of onion – they took turns talking.

'It looks as if there is something going on that I can't see,' said the lawman, stopping with a forkful of peas halfway to his mouth. 'Both men are from the same range over in California. Do you think the killer might be from over there? Followed them here to get rid of them for some reason?'

Matt thought about that for a minute, sopping up gravy with

a piece of thick sliced bread. 'Could be, I suppose. But the only men I've met have either been Nevada ranchers and the handful of cattle buyers, unless there's someone I took to be a local resident and isn't.'

'Well, from what I've seen, there aren't too many Californians come over. Harcourt indicated to me he was here representing a number of ranchers from over there. As far as I can see, the only strangers are that handful of ranchers from around here and buyers from farther east.'

For a while neither man said anything as they finished their meal. Matt used the time to consider telling the lawman what he was waiting for, but decided not to. That bit of information wouldn't help in the search for the killer but might muddy the sheriff's thinking.

'When are the railroad people suppose to be here, anyway?' Matt asked as he pushed the empty plate away, replacing it in front of him with a second cup of coffee.

'The way I heard it was that they would arrive in town on Saturday's train and meet with the cattlemen interested in shipping East. That will give the buyers for some of those markets a chance to get to know the ranchers so they have some idea of the kinds of stock that'll be coming their way.'

'This is, what, Thursday? Seems most of the ranchers took this as an excuse to come into town a day or three early.'

'Well, this is a slow time of year for them. Late summer, if they are going to drive up to the usual rail pens, their crews have already started. Most of these men, you'll have noticed, are older. Been ranching in this part of the country for a number of years. Now, I've never been on a cattle drive, but I'd imagine it's a young man's game.'

'Yeah. Well, that doesn't help us much, does it? The usual reasons someone kills are money or passion. Now, from what Miss Susan says, her pa wasn't carrying much money and old Howard had his funds on him when he was killed. Do you think his killer was scared away before he could find the money belt?'

'The clerk said he heard something fall, but finished with a customer before going up the stairs to check. He saw the door to Howard's room open and saw the man lying on the floor. He said he didn't see or hear any one.'

'That leaves passion and that takes us back to someone with a grievance against the two men. And that more than likely means someone they knew back on their own range.'

Blanchard fell silent, twirling a spoon on the table top with a finger. 'Or,' he started to say, then hesitated a beat before going on, 'or someone here. Someone who was so against this becoming a cattle shipping town they decided to take things into their own hands to press their point.'

Looking at the man, Matt grimaced. Or, he said to himself, someone looking for the envelope. Shaking his head, he glanced at the sheriff. 'Do you really believe the anger about this happening runs so high that someone would murder two old men?' he asked doubtfully.

The sheriff didn't respond.

'OK then,' Matt went on. 'Whom do you have in mind that this fits?'

'Damn it, I don't want it to be someone from town,' Blanchard said vehemently. 'These are good people. Yeah, there's a couple hot heads, like young Neely, and his father gets pretty wound up when he thinks he's right and everyone else is wrong. But still, they are good people.'

Again, silence settled on their corner of the room. While the two of them had been eating the rest of the small room had filled with men taking their midday meal but instinctively everyone, including the young man waiting on tables, left them alone. Now, noticing they were alone in the restaurant, Matt and Blanchard stood up, dropped a few coins on the table, and went out on to the sidewalk.

'I just don't know, Mr Kendrick,' the sheriff said, settling his gunbelt on his hips.

'Well,' Matt said with a nod while he carefully put his Stetson on, making sure it sat at the correct angle, 'one thing we can get straight.'

'What's that? How much you're being paid for helping me?'

'Nope. I'm not a badge-wearing kind of man, so while I'll help you as I can, I don't want a job. Pay me off with a meal or a drink now and again. No, what you can do is forget the Mr Kendrick. I'm Matt to my friends and, I guess, to the local lawman.'

Laughing, Blanchard stuck out his right hand which Matt, a big smile on his face, shook. 'All right, Matt,' he said, stressing the name, 'I can understand that. To tell the truth I'm a lawyer, not a badge-wearing kind of man myself. But someone had to do it, so here I am. And I hope, with your help, we can figure this out.' Smiling, he added, 'It'll help make me look good to the voters if I decide to run for some office later, such as county judge.'

Matt's smile faded a little. 'My reasons are slightly different. I think that pretty young Californian rancher should know that her father's killer didn't get away. Now, about payday for the hired help. In the mood for a drink?'

'No. I guess I'll walk up the street and stop off to let my wife know I won't be home for lunch. I'll buy you a drink later this evening.'

Settled comfortably against the mahogany counter, a glass of whiskey in one hand and the other resting on the bar, Matt thought about his new employment. His original objective had been to scout around the West to find something he could get involved with. His experience to date had been mostly as an army officer, his education focused on military tactics, literature and history. Nothing suitable for anything but army service, but here he was, in the West, mixing with cattlemen and the local sheriff. This wasn't exactly the way he had foreseen how things would turn out. Of course, there was nothing to say that this was the end of the road. Once he had been given the information that Colonel Cummings was after, and had handed it over, he was free to continue his search for his future. All he had to do was to wait until he was given that message.

'Hello.' A woman's soft voice greeted him. Matt had been so wrapped up in his thoughts that he hadn't paid much attention to the young woman. Her floor-length dress, of some pale-blue silky material, was cut low enough in front to leave the tops of her breasts uncovered. It was tucked in tightly at the waist, and she had caught his eye when he walked in, but only briefly. She had been standing next to a poker table, talking to one of the players. Now she was standing at the bar, next to him.

Matt had always enjoyed the company of women, and he smiled his welcome. 'I saw you when I came in but didn't think I'd be fortunate enough to catch your eye.'

'Oh, you're a smooth talker, aren't you,' she said with a laugh. Looking him up and down, she exaggerated her inspection. 'Not one of the ranchers, I'd say. Mmm,' she murmured, pursing her lips, 'and probably not a businessman. You carry yourself well, as a successful professional man would, but you're certainly not a doctor or banker or even a gambler. No, I'd say,' noticing the butt of his gun half-hidden under his coat, 'oh, either a lawman or a highwayman or . . .' she stopped teasingly, 'an army officer.'

Matt's reaction was to wonder if this woman had the information he was after. Then, realizing she was merely teasing him, he laughed. He liked her bantering tone. Returning the exaggerated inspection, he took his time to look her up and down.

'Well, the dress is very nice; the color makes your eyes much bluer. However, under that costume I'd almost swear there is a high-stakes poker player. A woman, obviously, with a taste for fine brandy, good food and liking more than a little excitement in her life. Not, I fear, someone who will be happy to stay home while her husband tends the flock and she takes care of fixing meals and ironing his shirts.'

The woman's smile, big and bright seemed to fade a bit as he finished his assessment. She wasn't as young as he had first thought; her skin was clear and more pink than tanned. Obviously she spent more time indoors than outside. Her hair, long and softly curled, was tied back, leaving her neck and shoulders exposed.

'Now, there I did it,' he said, letting his smile disappear. 'I went too far with my observation and said too much; your lively smile lost some of its glow.'

Shaking her head, she looked away and motioned to the bartender. 'Henry, will you pour me a glass, please?' Looking back up at Matt, she let the smile return. 'You were right, I do like good brandy and Henry keeps a bottle hidden under the counter for me. Would you care for a glass?'

'I'm afraid my taste is more for good whiskey than brandy, but thank you,' he said as Henry placed a small glass of dark brown liquid in front of her. 'However, I would like to pay for this.'

'It's not necessary,' she answered laughing. 'I own the saloon and am not in the business of letting the customers pay for my drinks. But thank you.'

'Ah, now that is the answer to every man's dreams: meeting a beautiful woman whose father owns a brewery. It is even better when the beautiful woman owns as fine an establishment as this one.'

'Well, to be honest, my husband and I own it. And he is not out tending any flocks, unless you call those men sitting at his table his flock.' At this she laughed again. 'That makes me think of our preacher, the good Reverend Neely, and his flock. I'm told that every so often, especially when he has nothing else to object to, he'll preach a sermon against fallen women. Not ever naming the one who owns the local saloon, but close enough for everyone to know who he's pointing his overly virtuous finger at.'

Matt joined in the laughter, thinking about how much

having this pleasant, intelligent woman in a saloon must irritate the self-righteous preacher. The laughter was interrupted when Sheriff Blanchard came pushing through the saloon's swinging doors.

'Come on, Matt,' he yelled, not coming in but hurrying back out. 'There's been another rancher bashed.'

CHAPTER 16

The man was in the back of the livery stable, sitting huddled in one of the last stalls. Typical of stables throughout the West, the building stood with large double doors open on to the main street with similar doors at the back. A series of pole corrals of various sizes backed up the barn. As he followed close on the sheriff's heels Matt saw a bunch of men standing around the last of the string of stalls.

He pushed through and saw someone kneeling over the man.

'Is he alive, Doc?' the sheriff asked.

'Yes, but not by much,' Matt felt the cold in the doctor's voice. 'I warned you, didn't I? Two men dead and now almost a third one.'

'Doc, I understand your opinion of the way things are, but right now I only need to know all you can tell me about this.' Blanchard turned to those men standing around, each trying to get close enough to see as much as they could. 'Get back, dammit!' he growled. 'This is serious business and I don't need any help from you all. Go on.' He let his voice harden. 'Get out of here before I start busting heads.'

Slowly, and muttering as they went, the men, most of whom looked to be locals, started moving away.

'Now, Doc, tell me what you can.'

The doctor stood up, brushed off his knees, and shook his

head. 'He's unconscious but his head is not bleeding,' Moser said, staring down at the victim and reciting the man's condition as if delivering a lecture. 'What blood there is isn't much, considering head wounds like that usually bleed a lot. His breathing is pretty steady. I looked at his eyes and they look normal, so there's not much chance he's suffering a concussion. He's not a young man, so that blow to his head is more serious than it would have been to you or me. I imagine he'll benefit from the sleep he's enjoying. That blow will give him a headache when he wakes up.' Moser looked up at the sheriff and went on, 'Of course, now that you've chased everybody off I'll have to go get someone to help move him.'

Matt's smile was slight as he heard the complaint. 'I'll go get a wagon. I saw one at the rail out front.'

'Bring a couple blankets if you can,' the doctor called as Matt walked back toward the front.

'Do you recognize him?' Matt heard the sheriff ask as he brought the small ranch wagon through to the back. He had found the wagon's owner just about to pull away when he asked for his help.

'No,' said Doc Moser, supervising the loading of the wounded man. Two saddle blankets taken from a tack room, covering a layer of straw, had been placed on the wagon bed to give the unconscious man some comfort. 'From his clothes, I'd say he was one of your ranchers, but I've never seen him before.'

After Blanchard had asked the doctor to notify him when the rancher regained consciousness, he and Matt stood and watched the wagon pull out into the sunshine.

'Well, there's not much we can do until he wakes up,' Blanchard said. 'That's all we need, another attack on one of the older ranchers. I guess it's good that he wasn't killed, but it sure is maddening.' He shook his head and continued staring toward the front. 'Maybe this time we'll get lucky. Maybe the old rancher saw something that'll help us. Come on. Now I think I need that drink.'

Matt stood still a minute. 'Something's not right,' he said. 'Whew! Boy, I know stables smell, but this is pretty bad.'

Blanchard turned back and looking around, nodded. 'Yeah, that doesn't smell like horses. The old man who runs this place is pretty particular about keeping it clean.'

'Here,' Matt said, kneeling near where the rancher had fallen. 'Someone stepped in what some dog left behind.'

He struck a match and peered at the brown mess that had been pushed into the straw that covered the floor of the stable. Abruptly he lifted his head and, curling up his nose, he exhaled loudly.

'Ah, that stinks. But it doesn't look like it was that old rancher who stepped in it,' he said, pointing. 'It looks to me like whoever did was wearing flat-heeled shoes, the kind someone from town, not a cowboy would be wearing.'

'I don't want it to be a local, dammit. Maybe it was Doc Moser who stepped in it.'

Matt frowned. 'That's easy to check. I'll go do that and take a look at what the old man's wearing at the same time. Here,' he said, picking up a pitchfork and scooping up the matted straw. 'Let me get rid of this smelly mess.'

He tossed it out the back, then stood for a minute looking at his horse, which was standing on three legs on the far side of a corral. 'Lazy,' he muttered as he walked back in. 'I need to take some time to ride him.'

'I think old Doc Moser would probably talk to me quicker than to you,' Sheriff Blanchard said as the two men walked out to the street. 'He doesn't know you from Adam. You go ahead and get those drinks poured and I'll go talk to the doctor.'

"Yeah. I seem to remember leaving before paying for my last drink anyhow. I'll meet you there.'

CHAPTER 17

'I didn't have a chance to introduce myself earlier,' the blue-eyed woman said to Matt when he returned to the saloon. 'I'm Mary Ellen McEwin. My husband,' she nodded toward the poker table which still had five men around it, 'is Mac McEwin. And yes, he's an Irisher and yes, he knows how many people don't like anyone from Ireland. To make matters worse, he's one of those very feisty Irishers, always ready to tweak someone's nose. I think that's why he didn't drop the "Mac" in front of his name when he got off the boat. To make it even worse, he took up the nickname of "Mac" just to rub it in.'

Matt laughed. 'I'm Matt Kendrick and I don't pick fights with anyone. It strikes me as strange that the good people turn their noses up at the Irish laborers while those are the workers who put down so much of the railroad tracks across the continent. They, and a lot of other foreigner workers, would do the hard work when the good people wouldn't. And as for fighting men, I had a lot of Irishers in my company during the war and I have to say, there were very few who didn't stand and deliver.'

Mrs McEwin's eyes sparkled with her deep-throated chuckle. 'My husband could be one of those. When he found work on the railroad it didn't take him long to discover that his skill with cards made more money than swinging a hammer. There I was, a young innocent girl in a small town when walking down the street was this big man in a sharp suit, hard derby hat and swinging a cane. Mama and Pa about had kittens when I told them I was marrying a railroad gambler.' She laughed softly. 'But here I am, not so innocent and still married to that gambler. Only now we own a pretty successful saloon. In some circles he's thought of as being a good businessman. Not, I'm afraid, by those attending the good Reverend Neely's church.'

Matt looked past the woman's bare shoulder and saw the sheriff coming through the doors. Blanchard tipped his hat to Mrs McEwin and he signaled to Henry for a drink.

'Good afternoon, Mary Ellen,' he said. He took a sip of whiskey, sighed and looked up at Matt. 'Well, our latest victim is still unconscious, but his shoes are clean. So are Doc Moser's.'

'Was he another rancher?' Mary Ellen asked.

Blanchard scowled. 'Yeah. We don't know his name yet, but he's not a local.'

'What did you mean about his shoes being clean?'

Before anyone could explain the doors swung open and the young red-headed son of the preacher stepped in. He stopped to let his eyes adjust to the dimness of the room, then looked around and, seeing the sheriff, headed his way.

'Sheriff Blanchard, I've been looking for you—' he started to say, only to be interrupted by the lawman.

'Jonathan Neely,' Blanchard said unkindly, 'you just interrupted a conversation. Whatever complaint you have can wait. As your father is so quick to tell me, my job is serving the local community and that's exactly what I'm doing.' Matt had to turn away to keep from laughing at the young man's reaction. 'Now, Mrs McEwin, as I was about to say, I wanted to make sure than neither the wounded man or the doctor had dog . . . uh, dung on their shoes. There was some sign that someone had stepped into a pile of dog droppings and possibly, if not either of those two men, it could have been whoever had struck the man on the head.'

Mary Ellen, glancing at Jonathan Neely, smiled. 'So now all you have to do is go looking for anyone with dog . . . um, dung on his shoes.'

Slightly embarrassed at the direction the talk had taken, Blanchard nodded. 'Yeah. Well, it's more information than we've had so far.'

'That's what I want to talk to you about,' Jonathan said, still standing in front of the three who were leaning against the counter. 'I have been arrested for something I didn't do and, while you've released me, there are still a lot of people who think I may be the killer. I want to backtrack that night, the night I got drunk and ended up in your jail. Maybe I can find someone who saw me and can help me clear my name?'

'You can start with that hired hand,' Blanchard said after thinking about it for a minute. He glanced over at Matt and asked, 'Do you remember what that drunk's name was, Matt?'

'Yeah, Barnwell, I think.' Turning to the young man, Matt explained, 'He works for a rancher named Russo. I haven't seen him in town since yesterday, but Russo's around, so I expect Barnwell is too.' Taking a close look, Matt saw that the preacher's son had changed. His face was no longer soft as it had been a few days ago. Still rangy, but now somehow more mature, it was clear that his brief time in jail had changed him. Or maybe, Matt thought, it was a mixture of getting really drunk, being thrown in jail and having to face his holier-than-thou father.

'I think you'll find that Barnwell will simply tell you what he told us,' said Sheriff Blanchard, 'that he heard you were in here the night before, drunk as a skunk and telling everyone that something needed to be done about the cattlemen and that you knew what that was. He said he'd heard that the night before old man Harcourt disappeared and just after his body was found. Now, you go right ahead and ask whoever you want whatever you want. Let us know if you find anything we should know,' Sheriff Blanchard finished, sounding almost rude.

For a moment Jonathan stood quietly, looking the lawman in the eye. Then, nodding curtly, he turned and, not acknowledging the other two, walked out.

CHAPTER 18

'Ah, hell,' Blanchard said, frowning into his whiskey after the doors stopped swinging behind young Neely, 'I shouldn't take it out on the boy, just because I can't stand his father. It isn't his fault his sanctimonious father rubs me the wrong way.'

'You were a little tough on him,' Mary Ellen agreed. 'What did you mean about Barnwell overhearing something on Wednesday night? If this man is who I think it is, he wasn't in here long enough to overhear anything.'

Both men looked up. 'What do you mean,' Matt asked. 'Barnwell is Russo's man. He was pretty dirty and looked like he had slept in his clothes the last time we saw him.'

'And that would be Wednesday night? About what time? I was here, as I am nearly every night from about six until ten or so, and he wasn't drunk when he took his bottle and left. That would have been about closing time, I think.'

Sheriff Blanchard thought back. 'We saw him the next morning in the alley next to the hotel. He smelled like a distillery and looked like he had just come off a week-long drunk.'

Matt laughed softly. 'Yeah, his pants were dirty and torn. Looked like an old pair of wool pants, so old that they might have been his pa's. And boy, did he smell. Reminded me of one of those moonshine stills I came across one time.'

'Well, as I remember, he wasn't wearing any wool suit when he came in here, but as I remember it, his shirt looked brand new. One of those cotton shirts with wide vertical stripes of bright colors. I remember because the shirt set him apart from his two friends. Except for his new shirt, he looked downright scruffy alongside those two, who were both dressed in more fancy clothes. One of them even had some small silver things decorating the sides of his pants. A couple dudes, I thought. But hard looking dudes, for all that.'

'Are you sure we're talking about the same man?' Matt asked.

'Well, I think so. Thin-faced man, needing a shave and wearing long black hair that needed to have someone take a pair of shears to? He had been in earlier that day with the two well dressed men. The three of them sat at one of the tables over along the wall. I didn't pay much attention, but they weren't here long, I don't think. I had come down to see Mac about something and took over the bar early so Henry could get home to his wife. He hasn't been married long and still likes to be with her as much as possible. That won't last long.' She laughed, then looked serious for a minute while she recalled that day. 'No, it was later, almost closing time when I sold that man the bottle of whiskey.'

Both men frowned. 'How long was Barnwell in here that night?' Blanchard asked.

'Not long. He came in and bought a bottle of our cheap whiskey. Paid for it and walked out. He didn't even have a drink. Just paid for it and walked out.'

'Well,' Blanchard said, finishing his whiskey, 'that certainly sounds like our friendly drunk. I wonder what that was all about? It'll be interesting, if our young friend Jonathan does find something we missed.'

The first people Jonathan wanted to talk to were his friends, the ones who had been with him when they had braced the cattlemen and his daughter in the street.

One, the son of the blacksmith, was busy working the big

79

bellows at the smithy. Not pausing from the rhythm that kept the forge fired hot, he listened as Jonathan explained what he was doing and what he wanted to know.

'Oh, hell, Jonny,' he said, lifting and pulling down on the bellows lever, 'we sat there and drank, the bunch of us. You did get drunk pretty quick, but hell's bells, you rarely ever drink with us. Not used to it, I'd say.' Laughing, he went on, 'I don't wonder you got so drunk so easy; I reckon that was really the first time you put down more than a sip of two of whiskey. We laughed about it after you staggered out. Hell, man, there was no way you could kill anyone and throw the body into the river. We were betting you wouldn't even be able to find your way home. You were drunk, boy.'

Feeling his face flush with shame, Jonathan mumbled his thanks and stumbled on down the street. Not wanting to face any more of his friends for the time being, he decided to go down to the river where the man's body had been found.

The Truckee River flowed fast and cold and he had spent many afternoons at a number of places along the banks, fishing for trout. One of the best pools was just downstream from the bridge at the end of the town's main street. Hunter's Crossing was named for Samuel Hunter. The old man had decided to leave the wagon train he had ridden across from Salt Lake City when he got to the rapids in the Truckee. Watching how difficult it was to get the heavily laden wagons across the fast moving water of the shallow stretch of the river, and thinking about the high mountains yet to cross, he decided not to go on.

Hunter had grown up on his father's farm alongside a wide, slow moving river and recalled how one man made his living with a flat-bottomed barge, moving men and freight from one side to the other. As he had come across on the Oregon Trail, before turning off on to the trail to the California country, he had seen that there had been other ferryboats to move each wagon across one river or another, each wagon paying a few coins for the trip. Below the usual fording place, Hunter had spotted a wide, deep, slow-moving section of river. There he would build his barge.

At first people had the choice of working their way across at the old ford, or simply paying the fare. People who arrived too late in the season to make it safely over the Sierra Nevada stopped along one side to spend the winter. In the spring, a few decided to remain and the town of Hunter's Crossing was born. Years later the bridge was built where the river narrowed and the ferry was put out of business. Now, the upper part of the long, slow, moving stretch of river was popular with fishermen or, in summer, for swimming. It was there that Harcourt's body had been dumped.

No one was around to point out exactly where the body had been found, but looking around the bank, Jonathan found scuff marks in the grass. This, he figured, was where the body had been pulled from the water. The ground was soft from recent rain and he could see heel prints from where the men had lifted the body. In one place he found cuts in the sod made by the wagon used to carry the dead man away. There was nothing to learn there.

Moving up stream a ways, he was stopped by a mass of thorny blackberry vines. A few weeks ago those brushy masses had been one of the best local supplies of large, juicy berries, most of which ended up in pies. Now, only the dried shriveled husks were left. Even the birds had given up on this source of food.

Shaking his head, Jonathan was turning away when he saw something sparkle in the thick grass. He looked closely, trying to find what had caught his eye. As he stepped back a little he saw it again: something shining in the afternoon sunshine.

He bent down, parted the thin grass and found a small, round, thin piece of silver. On his knees, he carefully searched the area for anything else. Finding nothing, he sat back and inspected the little silver button. It was distinctive, but he knew that didn't mean it had anything to do with anything. A lot of people had been here only a few weeks ago, picking blackberries.

Probably, he thought, glancing at the thick bush which grew in some places higher than any man, there were a lot of bits and pieces of clothing lost in there. The thorny vines, all interwoven so as to make a near solid wall, even hung out over the moving water. Looking at that, he noticed a few trailing tendrils bouncing unnaturally in the current. Careful of the thorns, he pulled on one. Whatever was on the end, it was too heavy to pull in but merely by putting more tension on the vine he felt the current turn and twist the weight on the other end. Revolving slowly, the wet, black, shapeless object came to the surface.

Careful not to lose his balance and fall in, Jonathan took another grip on the vine and, pulling gently, lugged the thing close enough to grab it. As he let the water drain out he saw he was holding a water-soaked felt hat. On the inner lining he saw the Stetson label. He brushed the hat off, gently pulled the pieces of green waterweeds that coated the crown, and discovered more sparkly pieces sewn to the hatband. Using his shirt tail to wipe the hatband caused the silver sewn to the band to gleam in the sunlight.

The silver pieces on the hatband were smaller and thinner than the button he'd first found, but were just as bright. None of them, he thought, had been where he'd found them for very long. This might be something the sheriff would recognize.

Jonathan brushed dirt off his pants and walked back to the bridge. He stopped there when he spotted his friend, Josh Moser, sitting on the bank, rubbing a shoe with a wet rag.

CHAPTER 19

'Hey, Josh,' Jonathan called out, happy to find another of his friends. He and Josh had been close for years and if anyone could help him remember what had happened that night, Josh should be able to. 'You're just the man I've been looking for.' He paused for a moment and frowned down at his friend. 'What're you doing?'

'None of your business. I ain't got time to talk to you now. Uh, I'm supposed to help Ma,' Josh said, standing up, 'so I'd better go on home.'

'Why are you standing there with one shoe on?'

'For nothing, dammit. None of your business, anyway. Leave me alone.'

Scowling, Jonathan looked closely at the shoe his friend was now holding. Josh quickly put the shoe out of sight behind him. Jonathan reached out and grabbed his arm.

'Whatever it is, you're sure acting strange. Come on, I'm your friend; what are you doing?'

'I told you, nothing!' Josh yelled, jerking away and nearly slipping down the steep bank. 'Dammit,' he cried, scrambling back up the slope. 'Leave me alone, will ya?'

'Something is going on, Josh. I don't know what it is, but somehow I don't like it.'

Angry and almost crying, Josh struck out with his empty hand. 'You don't like it? Who are you to like or not like? I'll tell you. I was only doing what had to be done, just like you did with that rancher.' The boy pushed a strand of his blond hair back with a finger he glared at Jonathan.

'What do you mean? I didn't do anything with any rancher.'

'Yeah, sure. You and your pa might have fooled the sheriff with that story that got you outa jail, but I know what you did. It was what your pa wanted you to do, and that's all I did.' Shaking his head, he scowled, his eyes filling up with tears again. 'But damn it all to hell, I couldn't even do that right. Some people can just do things and others can't, I guess.'

Seeing the question on Jonathan's face, he went on to explain. 'You and your pa are like that. Me and my pa, well we can't do anything. Your pa is well liked. Everybody in town respects him. When he says something, people listen. My pa? He's just as important, ain't he? He's the only doctor in these parts, after all. But no. It's only when people are hurting or gonna have a baby do they call him. So what that he drinks? Yeah, maybe too much, but that don't mean anything. He's still smart and knows a lot, but nobody even knows he's alive. And you . . . you're able to stand up and talk to the sheriff and he listens. He didn't pay any attention to me, did he? No,' he answered himself.

'You mean the other day in the street? You were there and you stuck your oar in the water and Sheriff Blanchard listened.'

'Did he? All I remember is his telling us to go home. He didn't hear a word I said.' Josh tossed his head angrily and brushed his long hair back behind one ear as he glared at his friend, who was looking once more at the shoe.

'And now you're cleaning the dog shit off your shoe.' As Jonathan looked up at his friend he saw his face go white. 'So it was you. You beat up on a cattle buyer to get back at the sheriff. Or was it because you think your pa isn't respected by everybody? I don't understand.'

'No! I was only doing what you did . . . what your pa said to do. We have to do what has to be done to get those outsiders out of our town. But I couldn't even do that right, could I? All I could do was beat up an old man.'

Jonathan watched as young Moser pulled the shoe on. 'Well, I did what I could,' Josh snarled. 'It's just like I said; some people can do things right and others, well, all we can do is try.' Head hanging and shoulders drooping, he shuffled quickly up the sloping river bank.

Watching his friend go, and thinking about all he'd learned, Jonathan decided he'd better talk to the sheriff.

CHAPTER 20

After hearing what Jonathan had to say about his friend Josh Moser washing his shoe off down by the river, Sheriff Blanchard and the young man had walked over to Doc Moser's house.

Jonathan tried to get out of going along but the sheriff wouldn't budge.

'Aw gosh, Sheriff, I—' Jonathan Neely started but stopped. He shook his head, and scowled. 'Sheriff, Josh has been my best friend for as long as I can remember. If he did what you think he did, well, some of the blame has to be put on my father. Maybe he's been too strong about what he sees as a danger to the town, but . . .' Once more, the young man stopped talking.

'Yeah. It doesn't look good, but we can't just let it go,' Sheriff Blanchard said softly. 'Now, it might be a lot easier for your friend if you're with me. Matt, you want to come along?'

Matt shook his head and watched the two walk away, one with his head hanging. Grimacing at the thought of what they would have to do, Matt turned and headed for the hotel porch. He didn't think he'd be needed and actually didn't like the feeling of being part of an arrest like that, so he headed back to his favorite chair on the porch. There were a few things he wanted to think about.

He sat with his feet up on the porch railing and watched as the night came on and lanterns were lit in those businesses that were still open. Most of those, he knew, would soon close up as the evening stretched into night. Remembering the conversation with Mary Ellen McEwin, he thought there was one thing he could do before it got too dark. He ambled along the porch and stepped into the dimness of the alley.

It had been two full days since he and Blanchard had been called over to hear what the drunk had to say, but hunkering down on his heels near that place, he could still catch the odor of raw whiskey. Faint, maybe, but it was still there. Matt struck a sulfur match and looked around where Russo's hired hand had sprawled. A dull shine a few feet off to one side caught his eye. He held the match higher and cursed as the flame got close to his fingers and burned him. He had seen what the reflected twinkle was, though: a discarded whiskey bottle.

He stepped over, picked the bottle up and, holding it at arm's length, frowned. Even that close, the bottle didn't smell as strong as the place where Barnwell had collapsed. Matt turned back, lit another match, knelt where Barnwell had been found and sniffed. The smell of whiskey was strong. He scraped a handful of dirt and weeds, quickly let it drop, stood up and carefully brushed his hands. Someone had doused the ground with the liquor.

Back on the porch he turned his discovery over in his mind. Why would Russo use his hired man to point the killing of Harcourt at young Neely? In telling the sheriff and Matt about finding the hat in the river, and handing over the little silver button, Jonathan had certainly got the attention of the lawman and himself. Neither of them had said anything, but both had recognized the silver button that the boy had found as being one of the conchos from the slick leather pants worn by Russo's foreman.

It was pretty clear what had been behind young Moser's attack on the old rancher, but what did Russo or his men have to do with the killing of the California rancher? And most certainly, whoever killed Harcourt and tossed his body into the river had also been behind the murder of the other one, Howard. Why? What did those two cattlemen have to do with the Nevada rancher?

CHAPTER 21

'One of the hardest things I've had to do since pinning on this badge,' Sheriff Blanchard told Matt an hour or so later. Most of the stores along the main street were dark. Only the sidewalk in front of the saloon down the street was lit up with lanterns suspended from the overhang. Light coming from the hotel and restaurant streamed out of the big windows, illuminating portions of the sidewalk in front of both establishments. Matt had moved his chair once, placing himself out of the light. Blanchard almost walked by where Matt sat in the darkness as he headed into the hotel. On hearing Matt speak the lawman pulled a chair over and sat tiredly down.

'Well, I guess it's been a long enough day. Claire will be wondering if I'm ever coming home.'

'There are a few things we should talk about, Sheriff,' Matt said, 'but I suppose it can wait until morning.'

The sheriff found his wife and Susan Harcourt sitting at the kitchen table with Ivan Russo when he got home.

'Well, good evening, Sheriff.' Russo smiled from his seat at the round table. The rancher had a heavy white mug in front of him, while the two women were drinking from thin, delicate china cups. While her husband seemed to live on strong black coffee, Claire Blanchard enjoyed her tea.

'Oh, Morgan. I hope you didn't miss your dinner,' Claire

Blanchard said, getting up and kissing her husband on the cheek. 'I was getting worried about you being out so late. We had heard about the poor man being taken to Doc Moser's. This is so unlike our town.'

Morgan Blanchard smiled reassuringly at her and nodded to Susan.

'No, dear. There hasn't been any more trouble. Fact is I just arrested the guilty party in that last attack. But,' he quickly added, 'we can talk about that later. Mr Russo, I have to assume it's not my wife's coffee or our company you're here for,' he said, letting his smile widen. Glancing quickly at Susan, he saw a faint flush spread over her cheeks.

'Morgan,' Claire admonished him. 'That's quite enough of that kind of talk from you, sir. That's so unfair.'

'Not at all,' he replied. 'Susan is living under our roof so we have to protect her interests, don't we?' He softened his words with his big smile. He went to a cupboard, found another mug and poured himself some coffee. 'Anyway, while my humor may be a little heavy-handed, I assure you it's well placed. More coffee, Mr Russo?'

'No, thank you,' the tall rancher said politely. 'My cup is still full. And yes, I admit to being here mainly to talk with Susan. Not,' he added glancing at the sheriff's wife, 'that having your company is not also enjoyable.'

Breaking her silence, Susan, still flushing a little, laughed. 'Somehow I think you are all teasing me. Sheriff, Mr Russo has simply offered me his help. I think that's very kind of him, don't you?'

'I don't mean any harm, young lady,' the sheriff said, taking a chair. 'And yes, it's a good thing to have someone there to lean on when it's needed.' He sipped his coffee and looked over at the other man. 'I don't mean to be too curious, but we don't know much about you, Mr Russo.'

Ivan Russo smiled. 'Just a bachelor rancher from a bit north of here. Actually,' he continued, seeing the interest on the faces

90

of all three, 'my operation is about sixty miles north, farther up along the Truckee River. Pa settled there about fifteen years ago. He and Ma staked out a section of land, most of it right along the river. We raise horses mainly, although since Pa died I've been trying to improve our beef stock.'

'I don't think I've ever seen you or anyone from your ranch down here before,' Sheriff Blanchard said.

'No. It's a lot closer for us to do our town business over in the little community of Truckee. We have a contract with the army for most of our stock, so it's not likely that we come down this way. It's the idea of being able to ship our cattle to Eastern markets by rail that brings me down this time, just like all the other ranchers.'

'I, for one,' Claire smiled, 'am glad you took this opportunity to come down to visit our little town. As my bumbling husband tried to say, we have gotten to like our house guest a lot.'

'Mrs Blanchard, I just wanted to let Miss Harcourt know that I am available to help in any way, if she needs me. I believe us ranchers have to stick together.'

'Why, Mr Russo,' Claire Blanchard said assuredly, 'I don't want you to think I'm being overly protective of Susan. She is, after all, a grown woman and now, with the death of her father, quite a wealthy one, too. You must admit that the attention you have begun showing could be seen as being questionable.'

Russo let his smile grow. 'Yes, I suppose so, although I assure you, I mean her no harm. It's just that she is alone now, and,' turning to Susan, 'I want you to know that I can be counted on, if needed.'

Russo picked up his hat from where he'd laid it on the floor by his chair, rose to his feet and smiled at the two women, as he shook the sheriff's hand.

'It has been nice to sit here and visit with you,' he said, 'but it is getting late and I must be getting on. Mrs Blanchard, Sheriff, I'll say good night. Susan, just let me know if there is anything I can do. Anything at all.'

CHAPTER 22

The next morning, while getting a haircut, Matt heard all about the arrest and jailing of Doc Moser's son.

'Well, ya know, I always did say there was something a mite strange about that boy,' one older man said. There had been three men sitting along one wall when Matt walked in. All were wearing typical town clothes: flat-heeled ankle-high shoes, pin-striped wool pants held up by suspenders and long-sleeved shirts of one shade of gray or dingy white. As he nodded his greetings Matt saw that none of the three was in need of a haircut. The hair on each head was for the most part thin and trimmed short above the ears. The man who jumped up from the barber's chair was mostly bald with just a fringe of ginger-colored hair circling his head just above the ears. He was the barber.

'Yes, sir,' the bald-headed barber said, whipping a tablecloth-sized sheet around like a bullfighter and pointing to the chair he had just left, 'a haircut this morning?'

'And a shave,' Matt said. He sat down and let the barber wrap him in the protective cloth. He closed his eyes as the man's scissors began to snip-snip, and let a small smile touch his lips. None of the three men sitting in the room had acknowledged his greeting by so much as a twitch. He wondered how long it would be before his presence would be disregarded and the conversation resumed. It didn't take long.

'Oh, I don't know about that,' came one voice, sounding fragile and almost weak, Matt thought, but for all that with a trace of authority sounding through. 'If any of the youngsters in this town is peculiar, I'd say it would be that preacher's son. Can you imagine growing up having to listen to your pa finding fault with everything but the sun coming up in the morning?'

Nobody offered an answer to that question and for a moment nothing more was said. Matt, careful not to move while the scissors were snipping so close to his ears, glanced into the mirror in time to see one of the men poke at another and catching that man's attention, motion toward Matt's back.

'Of course,' the man seated in the middle opined, gently stroking his mutton chop whiskers, 'I expect the blame for all this can be laid directly at the feet of those ranchers and cattle buyers.' He paused a minute and then nodded, as if in response to an unspoken comment. 'Yes, I know what you're thinking: having the railroad turn this fine little town into a shipping center will be good business. But quite possibly what we're seeing now is only the beginning of things to come. Don't forget, there's two men dead and another beaten up lying in bed over at Doc Moser's place. We've all heard what happens when drovers bring their herds up to Abilene or Dodge City. I dunno if that's not what could happen here.'

All three sets of eyes were focused on the back of Matt's head.

'Gentlemen,' he said, still not moving his head, 'I am not a rancher or a cattle buyer, so don't be trying to get a reaction out of me. If you want to start an argument, then it would have to be on the outcome of the war. I'm just recently retired as an officer in the US Army, just traveling through, and I decided to stop for a time. You can probably get a rise out of me if you're a Southern supporter, but as far as this becoming a hurly-burly cattle town, why, I couldn't care less.'

During the silence that followed, the barber put down his scissors, picked up a cup of shaving soap and started working up a lather. Brushing the foamy lather on Matt's lower face and neck stopped him from talking.

'You say you're not a rancher,' the third man said slowly. 'Then it could be that you're here looking for a place to settle?'

Not able to speak, and not even willing to nod as the barber finished stropping his straight razor and started to gently scrape off the thick shaving cream, Matt merely grunted.

'Well, now that changes things a mite,' the man went on. 'Old Samuel here is the local justice of the peace. He's retired, but still deals in land once in a while. All the land transactions have to be filed with the JP, you know, so he knows what's available.'

'Yes,' the weak-voiced old man said in agreement. 'There are a few acreages I know about. Of course, you could take yourself over to the office and go through the records yourself.' He hesitated a bit, then went on. 'But that would mean knowing something about which pieces of land are for sale. I guess, for a slight consideration, I could assist you in your endeavor.'

Having finished, the barber used the cloth to wipe the last of the lather from Matt's face and, after pouring a splash of bay rum in his hands, applied the sweet smelling liquid to his customer's face and neck.

Matt put the necessary coins in the barber's hand and looked at each of the three men. 'Well, I'm not sure this is where I'm thinking about settling, mind you. But I would be willing to pay for information, if I was to end up using it to find a suitable property. Tell me, are there any spreads north of here for sale?'

'North of town?' the man identified as Samuel asked slowly. 'No, I can't think of anything up that way.'

'I seem to have heard something about . . . what was that name,' Matt frowned, looking down at the floor as if trying to remember something. 'Oh, yes. It was Russo, or something like that. Is there a ranch owned by the Russo family on up north a piece?'

'Well, yes. Old man Russo ran some horses up there. That's

not in this county, though, so I don't know much about it.'

One of the other men cut in, 'I don't know if it's for sale or not, but I heard once that when the old man died his son took over and the place has gone downhill since. Seems the boy isn't as much interested in working the spread as his pa was. At least that's what I heard.'

'Well, then. It just might be possible,' Samuel said. 'I could ask around. The land office in Carson City would know and I could telegraph a friend about it if you'd like.'

Matt stood for a moment; then, making sure his hat was secure and at the right angle, he shook his head. 'No, I don't think I'll get too excited about it. At least,' he quickly added, seeing Samuel's face, 'not right now. I'll wait to see how this cattle shipping deal works with the railroad.'

He nodded to the barber and the three men and walked out of the shop. As he stood on the sidewalk he watched Sheriff Blanchard come down the street and turn in to his office. It was time, Matt thought, to go share some of the things he'd learned about the rancher Russo and his drunken hired hand.

CHAPTER 23

It didn't take Matt long to explain to the sheriff what he'd found in the alley by the hotel.

'So you think Russo's hired hand wasn't that drunk after all? Why would they go to those lengths to make us think he was?'

Matt shook his head. 'It does seem like a lot just to get us to go looking for the preacher's son. But if Russo wanted to make sure you weren't suspecting him, then something had to be done fast and possibly that was the best he could think of.' Seeing he hadn't totally convinced the sheriff, he went on, 'You have to remember, Jonathan found one of those silver conchos down by the river, right at the place where someone threw Harcourt in.'

'But send his man to get a bottle of whiskey and then wait until the next morning?'

'They waited until you were close by so he could get you to hear what Barnwell had to say. I have to think there's something going on with that rancher.'

'I don't know. He was over at the house yesterday evening talking to Claire and Susan Harcourt. He seemed just like what he said he is; a rancher from up north a bit.'

'Well, the fellas over at the barbershop didn't think he was quite the success at ranching that his pa was.'

'Have you ever heard any of the old men in a barbershop talk any good about whoever they're talking about,' Blanchard laughed. Before the two men could go on with their discussion they were interrupted by a man coming into the office.

'Sheriff? I'm Jacob Carlyle, the railroad official out here to meet with those from the Central Pacific Railroad to discuss setting up a shipping schedule,' he said, sticking his hand out towards the lawman. Carlyle was a young man, dressed in light-green whipcord pants and jacket worn over a tan cotton shirt. His boots were heavy-soled and the leather uppers were laced up almost to his knees.

Blanchard smiled and pointed to Matt. 'Mr Carlyle, there's a passel of men waiting to talk to you. Cattlemen and cattle buyers, all anxious to be using your new holding pens down at the station. This here is Matt Kendrick. He's been helping me on a couple of things.'

As the three men sat down around the lawman's desk Carlyle explained that he had just arrived in town on the morning train. 'Just in time to be given some bad news I'm afraid.'

'What we don't need is more bad news concerning the cattlemen and the train,' Blanchard said. 'Exactly what news was you handed?'

Carlyle waved his hand as if to downplay what he had to say. 'This isn't anywhere near that bad, but, well, it's not good, not by any means. I heard about the two cattlemen getting killed and the other beaten up. But what I learned, well, I'm afraid it could delay things for a while. Let me explain. It seems that the telegraph line from the California side is down.' He grimaced and shook his head. 'Now don't think I'm against the idea of linking up with the Central Pacific, because I'm not. But this does not surprise me. I think it was bound to happen. It's the fact that the Sierra Nevada mountains are so difficult to cross that worries me. If we are to set up a scheduled service, the CP will have to be able to guarantee they can maintain their part of things.'

'Does having the telegraph line down mean the Central Pacific Railroad is down?' Matt asked.

'Not by itself. No. But, well, it could be caused just by a break in the line or it might be something worse, a landslide taking out a section of rail. This is why I am a little apprehensive about getting the Union Pacific into any agreement.'

'What does this mean for the plan of making Hunter's Crossing a central shipping point?' Blanchard asked.

'Oh, that'll go through,' the railroad man said with assurance. 'The question has to do with setting the schedule. Both companies have to finalize their individual timetables, you see. Without our being in contact with Central Pacific's main office over in Sutter's Fort, well, I don't know how things can progress at this point.'

The three men sat silently for a brief time. 'Won't the railroad people on the other end notice there's a break in the telegraph line?' Sheriff Blanchard asked after a moment.

'I would expect so, but if the break is close to this side it'll take a while for them to get over to it. And if it's not just the telegraph wire that's down, if it's the rails that have been washed out, say in a landslide, then repairs will take even longer. That, I have to believe, is the case.'

'But,' Matt stressed, 'if it was just the wire, say a pole got knocked down by that landslide, then it could be fixed pretty easily, couldn't it?'

'Well, I suppose so. If all it is a break in the wire, it could be repaired in minutes.'

'Then until we know how bad it is,' Matt went on, 'all we're doing is worrying about nothing. Is there anything being done from here to find the break?'

'Well, no,' the railroad man said slowly, stretching out the word.

'Let me ask, Mr Carlyle,' Blanchard said, making his words hard, 'why not? It seems to me to be in the best interests of both rail lines to get this issue taken care of as soon as possible.'

Carlyle looked quickly from the sheriff to Kendrick, then, and seeing no help, let his gaze fall to the office floor. 'Well, yes,

I suppose. Of course, even if someone were handy, he'd have to go up the line to wherever the break is. That someone would have to know how to climb the pole and repair the break. It could still take a day or more.'

'Again,' Sheriff Blanchard cut in, 'won't it be likely that the California people will be sending out someone to patch up the trouble?'

'As soon as they know about it, I'd expect so,' Carlyle said, starting to sound weary of the whole topic.

'Mr Carlyle, be honest, is there someone down at the station who could make the repair, if they found it?' Matt let his voice grow as hard as the sheriff's had been.

'Well, yes,' the railroad man had a hard time meeting the other's eyes, 'I guess I could do it.'

'Then,' Sheriff Blanchard said, standing up and letting a big smile lighten up his face, 'I guess that the problem is on its way to being solved.' He put his hand on Carlyle's back and gently pushed the man toward the door. 'And once it's taken care of, I'm sure the district manager will be glad to hear of your efficiency.'

The sheriff opened the door and walked the man out, but stopped on the threshold. 'You're a good man, Carlyle. It is good to see the Union Pacific being so helpful.'

He closed the door and turned back to Matt, laughing. 'Poor bugger kind of put himself into a corner, didn't he?'

'Somehow I think he wanted to think the worst for the Central Pacific. If you hadn't pushed him, he wouldn't have moved a muscle to help.'

Chuckling, the sheriff agreed. 'I certainly don't feel guilty about it.'

CHAPTER 24

'Where's Barnwell?' Russo asked his foreman as Grogan came up to the table in the saloon where the rancher was relaxing. 'I think we should have a little talk. Find him and meet me in my hotel room,' he ordered, not giving the man a chance to respond.

Later, in the hotel, Russo sat on the only chair in the room and poured himself a drink from a bottle of whiskey. Grogan, having waved away the invite to pour his own, leaned against one wall.

There came a knock at the door. Before anyone could answer Barnwell came in. It was a different Barnwell from the one who had been lying drunk in the ally. Instead of being dirty, torn and smelly, the hired hand was now wearing the usual down-at-heel riding-boots, worn denim pants and a faded long-sleeved shirt typical of a cowhand. The only thing not usual for a hired hand was the holstered Colt hanging from a wide, thick leather belt.

Before Russo could say anything Barnwell started telling the two men about the telegraph being down. 'I was just down at the stable, boss, and heard someone say the telegraph line over the mountains is down. Seems there's a railroad man just got into town and he's getting ready to go up the line to see if it can be fixed.'

'Wonder if the break is on this side of the mountains? It

could be on the other, you know,' Russo said slowly, then added thoughtfully, 'I guess it doesn't really matter, though. Damn, that break in the telegraph line is good news, something I should have thought of.'

'What do you mean, boss?' Barnwell asked. He took up the open whiskey bottle and poured himself a drink.

'Never mind. And don't get comfortable. I've got another job for you. Get your horse and some grub. I want you out of town for a day or so. There's that old cabin up the river that looked deserted when we rode down here. Stay there and keep out of sight. I'll send Grogan for you and he'll tell you what I want you to do.'

'Aw, damn it, boss,' the hired hand started to protest but stopped when he saw the look in Russo's face. 'Ah, the hell with it.'

Barnwell quickly finished his drink, poured another, stood up and tossed it down. Then he settled his hat, glanced at the foreman and stomped out, slamming the door behind him.

'Damn fool,' Grogan murmured. 'I don't think he can be trusted to keep his mouth shut. What say I close it for him before someone gets him talking?'

'No. I have a plan for him, but that'll wait. Right now I want you to go through Kendrick's room. Life would have been a lot easier if you'd done as I told you and gotten rid of him on the train. I caught hell from the man in Washington who's paying the bill. He must have someone else here in town reporting to him.'

'I only had that one shot at the man. Like I told you, from then on he was too careful. Anyway, he didn't have any reason to think it had anything to do with his coming out here. I sure hated to lose that knife, though.'

'From what we can make from this deal, you can buy a dozen knives. Well, it's too late to worry about that now. Nothing has really changed. The main thing is we have to get the information about the gold shipment before he does. According to the man in Washington, there haven't been any signals sent from here so I don't think he has it but we have to make sure. Wait until he's gone to supper or something. I don't think you'll find anything, but it has to be done and I can't trust that damn Barnwell with it. I'm not at all sure of his judgement. The way you dealt with Harcourt was one thing. At least you were able to lay the blame on one of those town punks. But Barnwell messed up by killing that other old fool. It was a mistake and could have drawn attention to us.'

'Now's as good a time as any for that,' Grogan said, pushing away from the wall where he'd been leaning. 'You staying up here?'

'No, I think I'll go wander around and see if I can find out what's going on. Maybe stop by and talk with the sheriff. I've been trying to get close to the Harcourt girl and having the badge-toter on my side can't hurt. We can meet at the restaurant later.'

CHAPTER 25

Sheriff Blanchard had invited both Matt and Susan Harcourt to take dinner with him and his wife at the hotel restaurant that evening. As he sat back, savoring a cup of coffee, he told the two women about having talked the railroad man into going up the line to see if he could do something about the break in the telegraph line.

Susan put down her cup, carefully wiped her lips with a napkin and looked over at the sheriff. 'What about the train, will it make it over? I'd like to get this shipping business taken care of. I hope to get back home sometime in the next couple days. There is a big celebration at the capitol in Monterey coming up. It's the swearing-in of California's new governor. He was a good friend of my father's and I think my father should be represented at the event.'

Claire put her hand gently on top of the younger woman's when her husband slowly shook his head. 'We'll have to wait a while to find out, I'm afraid. That railroad official who came by the office said the break could be on either side of the mountains. There's no way of knowing. He's gone up the line to see if there's anything he can do. Until he comes back, we won't know just what the problem is.'

'You know,' Matt observed, 'that fellow Carlyle said he had expected there to be trouble on the Central Pacific line over the mountains. Almost sounded as if he was pleased to hear there was trouble with that company.'

'Well, there's probably some company rivalry at work there,' Sheriff Blanchard said, nodding in agreement. 'It could be like he said, a landslide knocking out the telegraph and the rails, or simply a break in the telegraph line. He did look to enjoy the idea of it being the worse of the two.'

'Oh, I hope it's only something with the telegraph line,' Claire said, looking at Susan, 'and not with the rails. That would mean you could return home. Not that I'm trying to get rid of you, of course, you are more than welcome to stay with us. We love having you. But I know how you want to get back to your home.'

When they had finished their meal, the four stood for a moment on the porch, enjoying the quiet of the early evening.

'That was a good dinner, Sheriff,' Matt said, settling his hat comfortably at the correct angle. 'And the company was the best part of it,' he said to the two women. 'And with that, I think I'll be heading down to have a nightcap with one of the owners of the local saloon. Good night to you all.'

CHAPTER 26

Hunter's Crossing was quiet the next morning. As men and women opened their places of business more than one commented on the quietness.

'Sure is nice, now that those out-of-town cattlemen have gone,' one apron-wearing man was heard to say.

Sometime during the night, a telegram had come in from the California side. Confirming the worse of the scenarios presented by Jacob Carlyle, a landslide had taken out a stretch of rails on the other side of the mountains. The telegraph line had been repaired but it would take the better part of a week before train traffic could once more come over the mountains. Final scheduling would be put off for that long at least.

When the news that any train traffic from the West would take a while, most of the cattle buyers had left on the Saturday train back to Carson City. The ranchers rode out soon after, heading back to their various spreads. Sunday, after church, the town dozed through the long quiet day, and now Monday was once again quiet under the morning sun.

The fact that most of the stores remained empty of customers wasn't lost on many shopkeepers, though. When the Reverend Neely happened in to Coker's General Store and commented how happy he was to be rid of the cattle people, neither Mr nor Mrs Coker nodded their agreement. None of those who bothered to take the time to sweep off the sidewalk in front of their stores paid any attention to the one stranger still in town. Late in the afternoon Matt Kendrick took his usual chair on the hotel porch.

Sitting with his hat pulled down to shade his eyes, he rested in the light of the westering sun. The only creature moving as the day wore on toward the supper hour was the black-and-white scabby-looking town dog as, with nose to the ground, it made its way down the street.

Enjoying the sun's warmth, he closed his eyes. Trying not to think about his failure to find the information the colonel wanted, he let himself doze off.

'So,' someone said, bringing Matt wide awake. He hadn't heard the sheriff come up and now the lawman stood smiling down at him. 'It must be nice, having nothing to do but spend the afternoon basking in the sun,' Blanchard said. He pulled another chair over and sat down.

Matt smiled and pushed his hat back. He took a long look up and down the main street. 'The town's certainly quiet today,' he said softly.

'Everybody went home as soon as they found out the railroads couldn't set a shipping schedule,' the sheriff explained. 'Even that old cattle buyer the Moser boy beat up was taken back home by some of his crew. That leaves me with two unsolved murders. With everyone gone, I doubt if we'll ever know what was behind it all.'

'Yeah, I guess so. But maybe your killer left town when all the buyers and other ranchers went?'

'Well, maybe.' Blanchard leaned against the porch railing, looking up and down the street. 'I would rather that than to find out it was someone from here did them in.'

For a few minutes neither man said anything, then Matt asked, 'Remember those ranchers saying they thought someone had gone through their rooms?' When the sheriff nodded, he went on, 'Well, I think my stuff has been searched, too. It's hard to say for certain, but it seems my saddlebags weren't buckled up like I usually do them. I can't think of any reason for someone to go pawing through my extra shirts and dirty laundry, but I think that's what happened.'

'Think you lost anything? Any money missing?'

'Nope, don't have much and what I'm carrying is all in my pocket. My extra Colt is still there, and so is the box of .44 slugs. No, as far as I can tell, if someone did go through my things, they didn't take anything. That's what makes it so hard to be sure. I suppose I could be mistaken. Just like those ranchers, I just can't be sure.'

'This whole thing is beyond me,' the sheriff said. He frowned and shook his head in disgust.

Matt nodded in agreement, then thought about the doctor's son. 'What'll happen to the boy, the doctor's son?'

'Oh, I doubt if much is done on that. He's really a good one, just got a little carried away. With his pa being the only doctor and on the town's board of supervisors, I expect the county judge will figure his time so far in jail is enough and let him go. It'll take a while, but the folks around here will remember that the old man comes from a ranch over closer to Carson City and doesn't trade here so they'll forget it soon enough.'

'I suppose if I was that old man I'd want my pound of flesh, but for someone that young, a few days behind bars will probably do a lot of good.'

The sheriff turned away from the street and gave Matt a long look over. 'With all the cattle people gone, you're about the only stranger still in town. Any plans on how long you'll be here?'

'I've been thinking about that,' Kincaid said, shaking his head and letting his glance take in the quiet street. 'This is a nice friendly town and I've been told there are a few places for sale, if I wanted to get into ranching. But no, I haven't quite figured out what I'm doing next. By the way,' shifting his glance up at Blanchard, 'it looks as if not all the ranchers have left town.'

The sheriff, following Matt's gaze, watched as Ivan Russo and his foreman, Grogan, came walking up the street. Russo was leading a beautiful black horse.

'You still think he's got something to do with all that trouble?' Blanchard asked as they watched the men continue walking toward them.

'I wish I could give you a reason for it, but yes I do. I'd still like to have some answers about that man's hired hand. The why of it all just doesn't seem to fit.'

'Well, I haven't seen the man the last couple days. Maybe I should ask about him.' The sheriff settled his hat on straight and stepped off the porch as the two men came up.

'Gentlemen,' Russo said. Glancing up at Matt he nodded his greeting.

Grogan, standing to one side, smiled up at the sitting man and shook his head before looking away. A ray of sunlight sparkling off one of the conchos fixed to the man's gunbelt caught Matt's eye, the black leather making the small silver discs stand out. Looking to see if any of the bits of silver were missing, Matt noticed that the foreman was carrying a rifle in his right hand. From where he sat, and from as much of the firearm that he could see, half-hidden as it was by the man's pants leg, it looked like a Spencer. Carried with the barrel hanging down alongside one leg, it had been overlooked when the men were walking up the street.

'Most all the other ranchers have headed on home,' Sheriff Blanchard said. 'They didn't waste any time hanging around once the railroad couldn't answer their questions. How come you're still here?'

Russo laughed. 'Yes, that's what old Grogan here has been asking. But then he hasn't been keeping company with that lovely young Harcourt woman, has he? He's right, of course, there's a lot of work back at the ranch to get done. I imagine we'll head out in the morning.'

'Talking about heading out, I haven't seen that other hand

of yours. What was his name? Barnwell?'

'We haven't either, Sheriff. He disappeared, what, yester-day?' Russo looked at his foreman, who didn't say anything in answer to the question.

'No,' Russo said. Looking first at the sheriff and then up at Matt, he scowled before going on, 'I think it was Saturday, the last I saw him. Barney hasn't been with us long and I do think he's probably got a drinking problem. I'll likely end up letting him go, I expect.'

Sherriff Blanchard frowned and kicked at a clod of dirt before continuing, 'Matt and I were just wondering, trying to figure out who would have a reason to go digging through some of the hotel rooms. Seems a number of the ranchers and even Matt, here, have had their rooms broken into. About the only fellow we couldn't place was your hired hand.'

'Now, Sheriff, don't go thinking Barnwell could be behind that. He'd have no cause to go sneaking into anyone's rooms. He just got paid not long before we came down to town, so he wouldn't likely be broke.' Looking up at Matt, he went on, 'You missing anything? Any cash?' When Matt shook his head, Russo looked back at the sheriff. 'I can't see Barney doing anything like that. But having said that, no, I don't know where he was most of the weekend, but he wouldn't have any reason to go breaking into anyone's rooms.'

'Well, if you happen to see him before you head out, I'd like to have a few words with him.'

Russo thought a moment, then took off his black Stetson and started to work the folds in the brim. 'Of course, Sheriff, I'll tell him if I see him before—'

His words were interrupted as someone came running out of the alley beside the hotel and slammed into the rancher, knocking him against the sheriff. As the man grabbed the black horse's reins from Russo and jumped into the saddle, Matt saw that it was Barnwell. Slamming his spurs to the sides of the horse and slapping its rump with his hat, the hired hand pounded down the street toward the bridge.

Russo picked himself up, stood for a heartbeat, then said quietly to Grogan, 'He's stealing my horse. Drop him.'

Quickly, in one smooth motion, the foreman brought his rifle up and without stopping to aim, fired. Matt was surprised when Barnwell, almost at the bridge over the river, was slammed out of the saddle and hit the ground flat on his face. The black horse ran up on to the bridge, slowed to a walk, then stopped to start chomping grass on the far side.

People, cautious at first, started out of several doorways, curious at the sudden rifle shot. Sheriff Blanchard and Russo took off running toward where the body lay, unmoving. By the time the two men reached Barnwell, others had already knelt down. They looked up to shake their heads as the lawman reached the scene.

Matt, standing at the porch railing, watched, then looked down at Grogan.

'That was some shooting.'

'Yeah. I've carried this rifle since Petersburg and I'm pretty good with it. Not quite as good as with a six-gun, though,' he snapped, his cold voice carrying its own warning as he levered another shell into the chamber.

'Good thing you had one ready. Barnwell might have made it over the bridge if you'd had to chamber a round.'

For a minute Grogan stared expressionlessly up at Matt. 'I find it always pays to be ready,' he murmured. Then he turned to walk toward the knot of men standing around the body.

CHAPTER 27

'He claims he couldn't let his hired hand steal his horse,' Sheriff Blanchard told Matt later. After Barnwell's body had been carried away and the crowd had broken up, Blanchard and Russo had stood talking for a few minutes. Shaking his head in disgust, the lawman had walked back to the hotel porch and taken a chair next to Matt's. 'I don't like it, but Barnwell had done just that, right in front of us all. Stolen the horse and was trying to get away. And, as Russo said, being knocked down was one thing but stealing his favorite horse was another. I still don't like it, though.'

Matt sat quietly for a minute then nodded. 'Yeah. It almost looked as if Russo's whipping off his hat was a signal. And Grogan was mighty quick and almost too good with his shooting. But you have to admit: if Barnwell had made it across the bridge he was gone. I asked Grogan how he happened to have his rifle and he said something about carrying it since one of the last big battles in the war. Somehow I got the feeling he was telling me something, but I don't know what.'

'Well, there doesn't seem to be too much that can be done about it. Whatever the reason Grogan gave for packing his rifle, Russo's horse was being stolen and he was in his rights to protect his property.'

'Funny,' Matt observed quietly, 'how just about the time one of us mentions wanting to talk with Barnwell about where he's

111

been the last couple days, he shows up only to get killed. Russo said he thought his hand had a drinking problem and was likely off on a drunk. I wonder if the pretty owner of the saloon can remember selling Barnwell enough whiskey for a two-day drunk?'

'Guess I could take a walk that way and ask. By the way, I notice you didn't join the crowd gawking at the body. Too far to walk?'

'No, I've seen plenty dead men before. The way he came face first off that big black horse, I'd didn't expect he felt anything when he hit the ground.'

'Yeah, that slug from Grogan's rifle did a good job on his back. Well, I hope that's all the excitement for today.' Blanchard stood up, looked down at Kendrick and smiled, 'And there we were, telling each other how quiet the town is.' He turned to step off the porch, then turned back. 'Almost forgot. I wanted to invite you to take supper with us. Claire's fixing something special and I'd like to show you how lucky I am to have such a wife.'

'I'd like a good home-cooked meal. Thanks.'

'You know, you haven't talked much about yourself, where you're from or even if there's a Mrs Kendrick somewhere back there. Now I wouldn't be so nosy, except those are the kinds of things my wife asks. Then when I say I don't know, she gives me that look that makes me feel like I missed something important.'

Matt laughed. 'No harm done,' he said. 'No, you can tell the sheriff's wife there's no Mrs Kendrick and I'm from . . . well, I guess my last home was with the US Army, which could mean anywhere back East.'

Blanchard smiled and nodded. 'I hear that since the end of the Great War there's been a lot of former soldiers from both sides coming West. With California opening up, I expect there'll be more than a few heading that way. Well,' he said, taking a long look up and down the street, 'I guess I'll have time to take another walk through town. Come on over about half past six.'

'I will, and thanks again,' Matt said, not making any move to get out of his chair.

The sun was just disappearing behind the false-fronted buildings across the street, but the warmth of the day was still pleasant. Watching the lawman walk away, Matt thought about the supper invitation. He'd have to make an effort to clean up a little, change his shirt and, he thought, running a hand over his chin, maybe even shaving. Yes, he mused, a shave would be in order, especially if that young pretty Susan Harcourt was still staying at the Blanchard house.

Thinking about it, he considered how much better the food tasted when there was a lovely woman on the other side of the table. Maybe that was part of what he was searching for. Then he went on thinking: about how impossible it would be to get a woman to agree to marry him right now, what with his having no business or ranch and only a horse, his Colt and a couple extra shirts to his name. A wife, he said to himself, was a long way down the list of things he was looking for.

There had been a few women over the years, but none of them had lasted very long. His working for Colonel Cummings didn't look like it was going to get him anywhere, either.

Colonel Cummings. That was what he should be thinking about, not a wife – or women in general. Matt had done what he'd been told, come to Hunter's Crossing. He'd made himself quite visible and had even become involved with the local law to give everybody a chance to pass on the information, but nobody had come up to him with an envelope, a message, or anything. The only thing that had happened was someone throwing a knife at his back, and that might not have had anything to do with anything.

Barnwell being dead meant he wouldn't be learning anything there. If Barnwell had been the intruder into his room, though, it was doubtful he was working on his own. Matt couldn't see any reason for the hired hand to go through anyone's room except to steal any valuables he'd come across. But nobody seemed to have lost anything. So, if the intruder *had* been Barnwell it could only mean he had been following someone's orders. The finger, then, just naturally pointed to Russo. But there was no reason for that, unless Russo was looking for the same information. Now that was a possibility. If the knife-thrower had been told to look out for him and Russo had had the rooms searched, it could all tie back into the gold shipment. Shaking his head, he grimaced, too blamed many 'ifs' to make any sense.

With the sun now out of sight, the long summer evening was quite enjoyable. As businesses closed and the shopkeepers went homewards, a few, walking past the seated man, nodded. One man offered his 'good evening' and a smile as he walked by. Matt frowned, trying to recall whose that familiar face was. It was the town barber. Matt hadn't recognized the balding barber because the man was wearing a hard derby hat. The greeting pleased him, however. After having been in town no more than a handful of days, he saw how easy it would be to become part of the community.

Greeted by the barber, invited to supper by the sheriff and who knew, he could purchase a business or some small ranch and become a valued member of the citizenry? Next would be finding a suitable wife and raising a family. That would mean a couple boys to take care of things when he got too old and at least one girl to make Mama's life easier. An old age when he could sit around the fire in winter and tell stories about how he had helped win the war. He could even end up being one of the three or four old men whiling away the morning at the barbershop, telling the others of helping the sheriff solve a couple murders during his younger, wilder days. Of course, whether from the boys at the barbershop or his grandchildren, the question would naturally be: who had been behind the killings?

Sighing, Matt decided it was time to go see about getting

cleaned up. The idea of spending the rest of his days here had about the same appeal as his staying in the army. But he would like to know the answer to the 'who did it?' question.

The Spencer carbine that Grogan had used so effectively, Matt told himself as he lathered up his chin, was something to think about. They were a pretty common saddle weapon, likely quite readily available since the end of the war. Captain Matt Kendrick had one of the newer sixteen-shot Henry repeating rifles in his saddle boot. That was the weapon he had heard more than one wounded Reb cursing as 'that damned Yankee rifle that was loaded on Sunday and fired all week'.

The .56 caliber Spencer with its shorter barrel was, on the other hand, thought by some to be the better saddle gun. Whichever, he said to himself wiping the last of the lather from his chin, that man Grogan certainly knew how to use one.

He donned his last clean shirt, which also happened to be his best, and a black string tie, brushed off his long suit coat and, after giving his boots a quick wipe with a rag, left the hotel. The walk down the street and then over to the Blanchard house wasn't far, but he took it slow, enjoying the cool evening air. He was smiling happily by the time he got to the white picket fence, feeling quite relaxed. As he walked up the brick path to the porch he almost laughed out loud, feeling better than he had in a long time.

A good meal of beef steaks cooked on the rare side followed by a couple glasses of Henry's beer was just about the best way to end the day, he'd said to himself. Well, maybe after dinner he would stop and get a glass or two from the saloon bartender. Now that was something to think about, too. Having dinner with two lovely ladies like Claire and Susan and then a drink in the same room with the lady saloon owner. A man couldn't ask for anything better than that.

It was Susan Harcourt who answered his knock on the solid wood front door. Even from the darkened front porch, the Blanchard house had the feel of being home. A slider rocker covered with pillows stood at one end of the porch and boxes filled with flowers, all giving the night air a sweet smell, were lined up along the railing. Warm, soft lantern light poured out of the curtained windows, laying a restful yellow cover on the porch flooring.

'Good evening, Mr Kendrick,' the young woman said, smiling up at him, the smile reaching up to her big, brown eyes. This, he said, was a woman who could get any man's blood pumping. 'I'm glad Sheriff Morgan and Claire invited you to dinner. The sheriff has been telling us about all the bad things that went on today, and we've decided that tonight we'll only talk about good things.' A decision Matt could only agree with.

He stepped inside and took off his hat. When she reached out for it, he gave it to her.

'Here, let me take that. Everyone's in the kitchen,' she added, pointing to an open door on the other side of the room. This room, he saw looking around, was obviously a man's room. A small fireplace encircled by river-washed stone and with a thick plank mantel above took up most of one wall. The furniture, a grouping of chairs and a long sofa, were made of similar dark, heavy wood, each packed with thick comfortable-looking pillows. A few mounted deer heads hung from a wall, their antlers spread out wide.

'Matt, come in, come in,' Sheriff Blanchard said, getting out of a chair and taking his guest's hand. 'Claire's been busy all afternoon fixing up something special. You're going to get better treatment than usual. We should have guests over more often, I suppose.'

'Are you complaining about the meals I fix for you, Mister Sheriff?' Claire Blanchard demanded, her smile taking the sting out of her words. A small dab of flour marked one cheek, left there when she had brushed her long brown hair from her eyes. 'I'm so glad you accepted our invitation. Poor Susan has been getting tired of just our company, I'm sure.'

'That's not true,' the younger woman cried out. 'Staying

here with you has been so nice. I only wish it could have been for other reasons.'

'Here, now,' Morgan Blanchard cut in, 'let's not forget our guest is standing there waiting for someone to put a glass in his hand. Matt, I've got a bottle of whiskey that you won't find in any saloon. Let's have a sip before dinner.'

What with the first-rate food and the congenial company, the dinner was almost enough to make a man wish for the married life. Claire had obviously worked for much of the afternoon in preparing the meal.

'I have to admit,' Matt said, finishing a second helping of her chicken that had been baked wrapped in slices of ham, 'that was about the best chicken I've ever had.'

'Oh, I imagine in your travels you've had better chicken suppers before,' Claire said deprecatingly but still showing some pride in his remarks.

The evening was, he assured the woman, the highlight of his stay in Hunter's Crossing.

'That's the truth,' he assured her. 'A great meal set right on top of that glass of wonderful liquor your husband poured, it certainly makes this an evening to remember. I suppose that I'll have to have a glass or two of the local beer just to remind my stomach that we can't live like this too often.'

'We can then take it for granted then,' Morgan Blanchard asked, innocently, 'that before turning in tonight you'll be stopping off for a glass or two?'

'If I learned one thing in the war,' Matt said with total seriousness, 'it is to not sleep on a too comfortable stomach. So, yes, I suppose the best thing for me is to do what I can to maintain my health.'

To the amusement of the women, the sheriff, mimicking his guest's somberness, nodded. 'I think I should get my hat and accompany you.'

Laughing, Matt thanked the women and said his goodnights. While Morgan was putting on a light coat and got his hat, Matt stepped off the porch and slowly walked down the brick path to the gate. Susan, leaving Claire on the porch, walked out to the gate with him.

Looking up at the star-filled sky, she sighed. 'The nights here are so much different from at home. Somehow the stars seem closer,' she murmured.

'Right now, with an evening with a good meal and warm company, it is very nice. I've never been to California, but I have to admit, the stars here seem bigger and brighter than back East.'

Susan laughed softly. 'You will have to come over the mountains and see what you've been missing.'

Matt smiled and asked, 'What are your plans now that the train will be delayed for the rest of the week?'

'Oh, I don't know. I did so want to return home early this week. I suppose I'll just have to wait until the track is repaired.'

For a minute the two stood looking up at the night sky, not speaking. 'This town will be poorer when you leave,' he said, and smiled at the blush his words caused. 'I expect more than one young male resident will start thinking about seeing what your side of the Sierra Nevada looks like.'

'All right,' Morgan said, coming down the path after giving his wife a peck on the cheek, 'let's go see about following the doctor's orders.'

Chuckling, Matt put his hat carefully on his head, closed the gate and followed the laughing sheriff down the street.

None of them noticed the man standing in the dark shadows of a nearby house.

CHAPTER 28

Ivan Russo waited, watching the two men walk down the street. As Susan turned back toward the house, and before she had reached the porch, the rancher moved into the street. He looked back, to be sure the sheriff and Kendrick were far enough away, then he called out softly to her.

'Miss Susan,' he called, keeping his voice low enough not to be heard inside the house. 'It's me, Ivan. May I have a word with you?'

'Why, Mr Russo, what are you doing out so late?'

'I was on my way to see you but saw you had company and waited. I didn't want to intrude,' he said, spreading his hands palms up to illustrate his good intentions. 'It is late and for that I apologize, but I've just heard some news that I thought might interest you. May we talk for a minute?'

Standing with one foot on the porch steps, Susan hesitated. 'I suppose so. Come up on the porch,' she said, leading the way.

Russo stopped at the bottom step. 'Oh, I don't want to take up any more of your evening. But I did remember our conversation and your concern about not being able to get a train home until late in the week. When I heard from my sister that she was going to join with friends from Carson City for the trip over the mountains to Monterey, I instantly thought of you.'

'I didn't know you had a sister. You've never mentioned her before,' Susan said, leaning against the railing and looking

119

down at him.

'I didn't? I guess it just never came up in conversation. But yes, Sophie is a little younger.'

'And she's going to Monterey?'

'That's when I remembered you wanting to be at the governor's inauguration. That's what Sophie and her friends are going over for.' He laughed softly, looking down at the ground. 'Of course, the fact that there's a young man in the party who has been courting her likely has something to do with her last-minute decision.'

'How is your sister's party going to make it over the mountains?'

'By carriage. There is quite a party going. They plan on making an excursion out of it, going by the Truckee Trail. It's longer and more gradual. The trip will take about three days to get across and then another day or so to get to the coast. Apparently there's quite a group of people going to attend the big celebration at California's capital city. Sophie said something about a dozen wagons in the outfit. What with there being some kind of problem with the rail line on the California side, this might be a lot quicker than waiting while things are being repaired. Anyway, I'm sure room on one of the wagons can be found for you.'

Susan was silent for a moment, thinking about the offer. She had heard about the Truckee Trail before. Branching off the Oregon Trail, settlers coming from the East had used it to get to California. Many, hearing of the warmer climate, turned off rather than going on to the Oregon Territory. It would mean a few days of wagon travel, but if she could join with the party Russo's sister was with, she would be able to get to Monterey.

'My father was one of the new governor's main supporters and, well, I would like to be there to represent our family,' she said, more to herself than to Russo. 'Are you sure it would be all right, if I become a member of that party?'

'I gather there will be a lot of young people going, so you

would fit right in. The only thing is, we are leaving early in the morning. It's about a day's ride from here to the ranch, but once we're there, you would have my sister as your chaperone. I don't know what people would think, your riding out with us to the ranch without another woman present.'

'Oh, piffle to what people think,' she snorted. 'But I don't have a horse and I do have two large trunks and a few smaller pieces.'

'Well, I thought of that. I can hire a small wagon from the livery to carry your belongings. If we don't waste time and leave early enough, we can be at the home place before dark.'

'Oh, that would be wonderful. Thank you for thinking of me and helping find a way of getting me home. I'll pack tonight and be ready first thing in the morning.' Her voice was filled with excitement.

'We'll be by to pick you and your gear up at first light. I'll have them prepare us some lunch at the restaurant so we won't have to stop.' Holding up a hand, he added a warning; 'the ride won't be as comfortable as the train would have been, but we'll get you there.'

'I'll be all right,' she said, wanting to reassure him.

Although sad that she would be leaving, Claire was happy at the news. Hurrying and giggling as if getting ready for a picnic, she and Susan spent the rest of the evening packing the trunks. Maybe, Claire said at one point, once the train schedule was confirmed, she and Morgan could travel over the mountains for a visit. She had always wanted to see what California was really like.

CHAPTER 29

The saloon was quiet when Matt and the sheriff pushed through the doors. They took a table along one wall, where they were joined by the lady owner, Mary Ellen McEwin. Enjoying her conversation and relaxing with their drinks, the two men settled back to enjoy the rest of the evening. After an hour or so, though, Matt started to feel uncomfortable with the beer on top of the big meal he'd eaten. Setting his half-empty second glass down, he said he'd had enough.

'I guess I will have to be satisfied with just one glass tonight,' he said, standing and giving a little bow to the woman. 'Ma'am, Sheriff Blanchard, I will wish you a good night.'

Blanchard sat a little longer, then he too left. At home he found his wife and Susan just finishing up the packing. Sitting at the kitchen table while they sipped a cup of coffee, he heard all about Russo's offer to help get Susan home. Not wanting to be a wet blanket, he waited until Susan had gone to bed before voicing his concerns.

'I'm not sure this is a good idea, Claire,' he told his wife as they prepared for bed. 'There's something not exactly right about Russo and his foreman. Both Matt and I are almost certain that those two had something to do with the trouble we've had in town this past week or so.'

Instantly Claire was concerned. 'What do you mean? Do you think he had a hand in Susan's father getting killed?'

122

'Well, not directly maybe. But that foreman of his, Grogan, we think he was by the river where her pa was thrown in. We just can't figure out why either of them would want to kill a couple old ranchers. On one hand, it looks like Russo and his men could have done it, on the other, there's no proof and no reason behind them doing it. Somehow, it just doesn't seem right.'

Lying back with his hands behind his head, he frowned. 'I guess Susan's all excited about getting back home?'

'Yes, especially about not missing the big affair at the governor's mansion in Monterey. With the train not making it over here for who knows how long, going by wagon with Russo's sister seemed like a godsend. We got her all packed up and she'll be ready to go when they bring the wagon by in the morning.'

'I still don't like it, but without some kind of proof, I don't suppose there really isn't anything we can do. Try to warn her to keep on her guard, at least until she joins up with Russo's sister. It's that Grogan that I really don't like the looks of.'

'Go to sleep. Worrying about it won't change anything or help anyone. She wants to be in Monterey in time for the big event, so we'll just have to keep our worries to ourselves. No reason to upset her.' Claire was silent for a while, then, not even sure her husband was still awake, she murmured softly, 'but I am going to miss her.'

Jonathan Neely left his father's house right after breakfast. He and his father had argued the night before and he didn't want to have it all start up again, so he left before the Reverend Neely had gotten up.

The issue was whether Jonathan would follow in his father's footsteps and become a dedicated man of God.

'This is your destiny, boy,' the elder Neely had said more than once. 'My good friend, Reverend Collinsworth, has agreed to have you stay at his home in St Louis while you attend the Baptist Academy. This is, I must say, very good of him and if you turn him down, why, it would be an insult. Living under his roof while you attend seminary classes will stand you in good favor. He is very well thought of in that community and your future will be assured because of it.'

Jonathan had tried to explain that it wasn't the idea of taking up the offer of housing; it was that he didn't want to become a preacher.

'How can you not?' Reverend Neely thundered. Often through the years, Jonathan had wondered whether his father's voice had always been strong and powerful, or was that part of what being a preacher was all about? Was having a certainty about everything something they taught at the academy? If it was, Jonathan was in trouble. His voice was never commanding and he was never sure about anything. Whenever he tried to sound like his pa, the words came out thin and high-pitched; almost, he thought, squeaky.

Anyway, becoming a preacher wasn't what he wanted. Actually, the only time he felt happy was when he was working outside. The only job he'd ever had was one time working at one of the ranches during a round-up. That had lasted one fall and when he had tried to hire on the next spring, his father had told the rancher that his son was not available.

'No son of mine is going to be a forty dollar a month cowhand,' the Reverend Neely had lectured the boy. 'Cowboys, by their very nature, are coarse, foul-mouthed and uncouth. It is, I'm sure, due to their living and working outside the civilizing structure of a genteel society. I won't have my son destroy his life.'

This wasn't how Jonathan saw it. Being outdoors, with no one to control his every waking moment, had been like coming into the bright sunshine after a night spent in a dark, dank cave. Those few weeks of riding night watch, fetching wood for chuck wagon fires and scrubbing pots and pans for the cook had been hard work. They had also been, for the first time in his life, a time of feeling good about his tiredness, his sore hands and stiff muscles. Being yelled at by the old, grumpy cook was one thing; being commanded by the authoritarian voice of his father was another.

Susan Harcourt was another factor in his consideration of his future. She had been on his mind since the first time he saw her. Angrily kicking a rusty tin can as he walked down the street toward the river, he felt his face flush with shame when he remembered the first time he'd seen her. She had been standing on the hotel porch with others as he followed his father home after being released from the jail. They had never been introduced, but he knew who she was. He had tried to tell her he had nothing to do with her father's death, but he could tell she didn't believe him.

On down the street his father had rebuked him for speaking to her as he had. For a time, Jonathan wasn't sure whether even his own father believed he was innocent. Proving his innocence became more important than anything. He had to be able to look Susan Harcourt in the face and know she didn't accept as true what he'd been accused of.

As it had done for as long as he could remember, the river flowed slowly by, gurgling sounds coming as the water poured over the last of the rocky rapids upstream, silent in the almost unseen movement below the bridge. Jonathan picked up a handful of small rocks and he began tossing them out into the water, watching the ripples disappear nearly as fast as the rock as the current flowed downstream.

With his home life as it was, he knew he'd have to decide soon, once and for all, what he should be doing. If he stayed here in Hunter's Crossing, some people would always see him as poor Reverend Neely's son. His father would not accept his decision not to follow in his footsteps, so really, leaving was the only choice he had.

Talking about his problem with his father just wasn't possible. When he thought about it, the only man he knew he could go to for advice was the sheriff. Since coming to town, Sheriff

Blanchard had always seemed to be friendly and he had more knowledge about life outside this town. Or maybe even that other man who was with the sheriff a lot, Matt Kendrick. People weren't sure why that man was in Hunter's Crossing, but Jonathan had heard that the big man had been in the Union army. Maybe he would be someone he could talk to.

As if part of the question had been solved Jonathan dropped the rest of the handful of rocks, brushed off his hands and turned back toward town. It was quite possible that either of the two men would be having coffee at the restaurant. As he walked up the street, he thought about what he was going to say.

Jonathan cut across the main street and walked up the side street on which stood the Blanchard house. Since hearing that Susan Harcourt was staying at the sheriff's house, he had walked along that street a couple times, hoping to catch the young woman out in the yard. Until today he had not been so lucky. This morning, however, as soon as he turned on to the street he saw a woman out by the porch, cutting roses off a bush.

Feeling moisture on the palms of his hands, he brushed them on his pants and hurried up the street. Disappointment filled him when he saw that the woman was the sheriff's wife, not Susan.

'Good morning,' Claire Blanchard said, looking up as he slowed his walk past the white picket fence. 'Aren't these roses beautiful?' She held the flowers out for his inspection. 'This bush is just covered with them, and if I cut them even more grow.'

Not knowing what to say, Jonathan was quiet as he looked at the bright red flowers she held out.

'I wonder if your father would like some for the church? They would look quite nice up by the lectern when he gives his sermon next Sunday.'

Jonathan nodded. 'I suppose,' was the best he could think of saying.

'Oh, this is a wonderful morning,' Claire went on, overlooking the younger man's silence. 'Usually I'm not out so early, but with everything happening this morning, well it was just too nice to go back inside.'

'What happened this morning,' Jonathan asked, afraid that there had been another bashing or killing. Things around town had been quiet since the ranchers and cattle buyers had left. His father, very sure that the landslide that had halted train traffic coming from over the mountains was a sign from his God, had been very pleased with the return of peace to what he considered to be his town. Another killing would prove him wrong.

'Susan's leaving. She left early this morning, you know.'

Crestfallen, the young man could only shake his head. 'No, I didn't know. I thought she was going to have to wait until the tracks had been repaired.'

'Yes, and that did disappoint her. She wanted to get home so badly. I suppose her visit here to Hunter's Crossing wasn't a happy time for her, what with her father being murdered and all.'

'How did she leave if the train isn't running yet?'

'Oh, that rancher from up the river, Russo, rented a wagon and took her up to his place. His sister is part of a party of people from Carson City going over the mountains by wagon and Susan is going to join that group.'

Jonathan didn't know the man, Russo. He'd heard someone over at the barbershop say he had a horse ranch somewhere farther up the river. Another man sitting in a chair on the porch outside the barbershop had only snorted.

'Ha, that's what you know,' the old man had said. 'His pa, now, he was a rancher, but the young Russo? All he knows is how to make trouble, him and that so-called foreman of his. Nosiree, ain't much those two haven't tried to get away with.'

'There you go again, sounding like you know a lot more'n the rest of us,' another man had said.

'Wal, maybe I do. Young Russo does all his business over in Carson City. Don't know why he came over here. From what I heard he ain't got enough cattle to call it a herd, so he couldn't be much interested in what any of those buyers from the East would have to say. Nope, you go up to Carson City and mention his name and you'll see. Nothing but a troublemaker, that's what you'll find out.'

Jonathan, standing in the sunshine just around the corner, had smiled, listening to the old men gossip. He sure wished his pa was like those men, all happy and joking among themselves. For certain, the fact that the rancher they were talking about didn't attend his pa's church meant his pa wouldn't even take the time to talk about him.

Now, thinking about Susan Blanchard riding off with the man the old men said was a troublemaker, worried him. Dejected by the news, Jonathan could only offer the sheriff's wife a half-hearted smile as he moved on down the street.

CHAPTER 30

Not finding the lawman or Mr Kendrick in the restaurant, Jonathan headed across the street to the sheriff's office. That too, he found, was empty. His morning was turning into a series of let downs. Seeing the barber and a few others sitting outside the barbershop, he went back across the street to ask if they knew where the sheriff was.

'Nope. Ain't seen him or that other fellow all morning,' the balding man said, getting nods from the other old men.

'I did see him walk over to the restaurant early,' one of the old men sitting in the morning sun next to the barber offered.

'Well, I looked over there,' Jonathan said. 'Guess I'll have to look for him later today. Thanks.' He waved his goodbye and started walking slowly on down the street.

'Hey, Richards, about what time was it you saw him?' the barber asked.

'Oh, real early, just a mite after sunup. I was just coming down the street after having my breakfast. It was about the time that Russo boy was leaving. Russo rented a wagon, you know.'

Jonathan, hearing Russo being mentioned, turned back. Not wanting to interrupt, he waited as the men ignored him and talked among themselves.

'Yep, I seen him heading down the street in one of the livery's rental wagons,' the man called Richards said, conscious of the young man standing with his hands in his pockets. That was one thing he'd been taught as a boy, not to stand around with your hands in your pockets, especially when in the company of your elders. No sir, the old man mused, his father, long dead now and thank God for that, wouldn't have allowed any of that kind of thing. No sir, if you got time to stand around, he remembered his pa saying, you got time to be put to work. That work could be anything from mucking out the stalls over at the livery or whitewashing the corral fences out back.

That was what his pa had been doing the day he keeled over dead, brushing a coat of watered down white paint on the corral rails. Well, for one, he didn't miss the old man. Shaking his head at the memory, he thought about what he'd been saying.

'Don't know why he'd want a wagon, though,' Richards went on, almost talking to himself. 'Had his horse tied on to the tailgate, all saddled up, too. And that foreman of his was riding alongside. Who knows what those two are up to?'

'He's taking Susan Harcourt up to his ranch,' Jonathan said, hoping to learn more about Russo.

'Susan Harcourt,' another of the old men said, his words coming slowly as if he was having trouble remembering something about the name. 'Oh, yes, that's the daughter of that rancher from over in California. You know, the one that was murdered and his body tossed into the river?'

Luke Masters, being the town's only barber, was conscious of his position. After all, every bit of gossip that came in the door was almost as valuable as the few dollars he made cutting hair. Maybe there was something here, he thought, suddenly remembering that the Reverend Neely's boy had been held by the sheriff for that killing. Trying not to be obvious, he looked sideways to see how the boy would act at hearing Richard's words. He was disappointed at seeing young Neely not react, so he decided to pick at him a little.

'Seems funny, those two old men getting killed and our

young sheriff not able to catch whoever did it. He had you in jail for a while, didn't he?' he asked, looking up at the young man.

Jonathan saw how all three men were watching and waiting for him to answer. Damn old busybodies, he thought. Just sitting in the sun gossiping about things they didn't know anything about.

'Yes, I spent a few hours in a cell over at the sheriff's office.' He smiled at the men drily. 'But when he found out I couldn't have been in two places at one time, the sheriff had to let me go.'

'Well, someone had to do it,' the man the barber had called Richards said slowly. 'I guess it was one of those fellas what was here to see about shipping their stock on the railroad. They've all gone now, so we'll never know who done it, I expect.'

Jonathan wanted to get the conversation back to Russo but couldn't see how to do it. After a minute or two of silence, the barber solved the problem.

'That was about the first time old man Russo's boy has come down here to the Crossing, isn't it?'

'Well, he don't come here very often, that's for sure,' one of the others said. 'Old man Russo done his shipping from Carson City, and after he passed on his boy continued doing the same. It's a mite closer, I think.'

Leaning against the rough unpainted pole that held up the wooden overhang shading the porch, Jonathan was about to ask something about how far the Russo ranch was from town when the barber again stepped in.

'I guess. As I recall their spread's a good day's travel up the river, ain't it?'

'Oh, I 'spect it's a mite closer than that on horseback,' Richards offered. 'Driving a herd would take longer, of course. I remember Pa buying a couple horses from the old man. They was for renting out to folks wanting to use one of the buggies we had then. Pa and I rode up and stayed in the bunkhouse over night. Brought them back the next day. Horses weren't no good, as I recall. Hard-mouthed and feisty whenever it got cold. Ornery old things. Don't know what Pa finally did with them. Probably sold them off to someone, I suppose.'

'I remember your pa, Richards. He was as tough as an old boot. Made the livery stable pay, though. You did all right when you sold out a few years ago,' teased the barber.

'Yep, I got a good deal, that's no secret. I won't ever have to worry who's gonna pay for my whiskey, and there ain't every old coot in this town that can say the same. And that's for sure,' he snapped, looking sideways at the other men.

'Wonder why the Russo boy wanted a wagon,' the one man who had been sitting quietly said reflectively. 'Seems it'd only slow him down going home.'

Jonathan responded before anyone else could. 'Miss Harcourt is planning on joining in on a party that's going over the mountains to California. She didn't want to wait for the repairs to the tracks up on the mountain to be finished.'

'That's young people today, always in a hurry to get some place,' Richards said disgustedly.

'I don't know, though,' Luke observed critically. 'If it was my daughter I wouldn't like it for her to go traipsing off with a couple men, like that.'

Coming quickly to her defense, Jonathan pointed out how there was a chaperone at the Russo ranch. 'She'll be all right, riding in the wagon up to the Russo place. That's what the sheriff's wife told me. The wagon was to carry Miss Harcourt's trunks. And then there's Russo's sister at the ranch. It's her party that's going over the mountains.'

'Hmm,' Richard said slowly, a frown on his face as he tried to remember. 'I don't recall there being any daughter. Russo's wife, as I heard it, she died when the boy was born. The old man had a woman friend over in Carson City he'd go visit, but he never did take another wife. No,' he said with some assurance, 'there was only the boy there when the old man passed.'

'Wait a minute,' Jonathan asked anxiously, 'are you sure Russo doesn't have a sister?'

'Not that I ever heard of, there ain't,' Richards said, nodding his head.

Jonathan stood thinking for a minute. 'Where exactly is the Russo spread?' he asked the men.

'Oh, like I said,' Richards offered, his words coming slow and deliberate. 'North a good day's ride along the river, I'd say. Can't miss it, long as you stay on the main trail. There's one fork in the road, but that's only a track out into the sage. There's an old sheepherder living out there somewhere.'

'Naw,' one of the others said, 'I heard that that sheepherder left the country a couple years ago. . . .'

Jonathan didn't hear the rest of the comment. He jammed his hat firmly on his head, turned and ran down the street to the nearest hitching rail, where someone had tied a black mare.

'Why, there you go,' Richards interrupted his story about the sheepherder, 'just like most youngsters today, just run off without a by-your-leave.'

As Jonathan jerked the mare's reins loose and jumped into the saddle, the barber stood up to watch him slap the horse into a gallop down the street.

'Say, wasn't that Herb Bonnet's horse? Boys, I think our young friend just stole a horse.'

CHAPTER 31

It took a while for the barber, Richard and the others to decide whether the Reverend Neely's boy had actually become a horse thief or not. Because he was a little younger than the others and as the only one of the porch-sitting gang actually to have a profession, the barber's conclusion on things was usually the accepted version. This time, however, even slow talking Richards argued that the boy had simply taken the first horse he'd come to and had ridden out of town. If that, he stated with some intensity, wasn't stealing then nothing was.

This discussion took the better part of an hour, so the first Sheriff Blanchard heard about the incident didn't come until all the dust had settled and the horse thief was long gone. After eventually agreeing that the incident might be something the sheriff should know about, they had to decide who would go over and report it. Luke, being the barber, and Richards, being the oldest, were chosen to do the job.

'Now, you boys slow down and tell us what this is all about. You're saying Jonathan Neely stole Bonnet's mare?' The sheriff and Matt Kendrick had been down at the telegraph office. Matt had attempted to contact Colonel Cummings back in Denver to find out what he should do. The colonel wasn't in his office but Matt was assured his telegram would be delivered as soon as possible. Blanchard, having little else to do, had gone along hoping to get some news about the landslide. Work on repairing the track on the California side was progressing, he was told. The manager of the Union Pacific said he'd been told it would still take the rest of the week.

Sheriff Blanchard had told Matt about Susan's decision to join the Russo girl's wagon party. Both of them had decided it wasn't a good idea, but there was little they could do about it. Blanchard had hoped to be able to find some good news about the arrival of the Central Pacific train; news he could take back to the young woman. They were met back at the sheriff's office by the two old men.

'Well, Sheriff,' Richards strung his words out in his slow manner, 'it seemed funny to us. You know, we was just sitting and jawing, when that young Neely boy came by. He'd been looking for you. Said he had something to talk to you about. Dunno what it was, he never did say, did he, Luke?'

'Nope, never did. I guess whatever it was would keep.'

'Was that when he took Bonnet's horse?' Matt asked gently. Somehow he couldn't see the preacher's son as a horse thief and was actually trying not to laugh at the story these two old-timers were bringing to the law.

'No. We was talking about that California rancher's daughter riding off with Russo and his foreman. Young Neely seemed to know a bit about that, told us how she was going to hitch a ride with some folks from Carson City who was going over the mountains. Well, that's what he told us, anyhow. Seems the girl was to travel with some sister of that fella, Russo.'

The barber, frowning at the way Richards was telling the story, cut in. 'It was when someone, Richards, I think it was you, wasn't it? who said Russo didn't have any sisters? When the Reverend's boy heard that, was when he took off like his pants was on fire.'

'What'd you mean, Russo doesn't have a sister?' Sheriff Blanchard came out of his chair.

'Not so's you'd notice,' Richards said, pleased that he'd been able to get everybody's attention. 'No brothers or sisters.

135

Old man Russo's wife died when the boy was born and he never did find another.' Scowling and looking down at the floor as he tried to remember, he muttered to himself, 'Dang it, I can't recall her name.'

Blanchard glanced at Matt, who wasn't paying any attention to the old man's comments. 'Now that doesn't make sense. Why would Russo tell a lie like that?'

Matt Kendrick shook his head. 'We've said all along, there was something funny about him and his crew. Having Grogan shoot Barnwell before we got to question him and now this makes me think it's all part of the whole thing, starting with the killing of those two ranchers.'

'And Jonathan went after them.' Blanchard grabbed his hat and turned to Luke and Richard. 'You tell Bonnet that he'll get his horse back. Jonathan just borrowed it. Come on, Matt. Let's go see what we can find out. If we let anything happen to that girl my wife'll have me skinned alive.'

CHAPTER 32

At first conversation between Susan and Ivan Russo flowed. Leaving town as early as they had, she had bundled up in a blanket loaned to her by Claire Blanchard. It grew warmer as the sun climbed in the morning sky and she studied the passing country with interest. For the first few hours Russo answered her questions and told her about life in the dry sagebrush-covered land they were riding through. Grogan rode silently behind the wagon, keeping off to one side out of any dust thrown up by the wheels.

'This is certainly different,' she said more than once, looking out over the brown landscape. 'I can't see how anyone could raise a herd of cattle out here. It's so, well, so barren.'

Ivan laughed. 'Yes, it isn't anything like I hear the valleys are over in California. Here, you get away from the river and there isn't much feed for man or beast. Those mountains over there,' he nodded westward, 'they stop a lot of rain from getting over to this side. We can't raise as many head per acre as you folks can, but with a little water pumped up from the river, we can do all right.'

For miles, as the wagon moved along, she didn't see any sign of there being a cattle ranch. No fences or water holes, and certainly no houses, or tracks turning off to some out of sight homestead. Coming up on a low rise, she felt she could see for ever in nearly all directions. And wherever she looked all she

137

saw was emptiness.

'There aren't even any wild animals. I don't think I've seen one deer or even a squirrel since we left town.'

'Oh, if you look closely, and know what to look for, you'll see some wildlife. Look,' he pointed over the horses' rumps with a gloved hand, 'see that ridge over there?'

'The one with the tall bush standing all alone?'

'That, young lady, is a tree. But yes, that one. Now you watch those little brown and gray lumps around it carefully. We get a little closer and they'll disappear.' Turning back to his foreman, he pointed and yelled an order.

'Grogan, we get close enough, see if you can hit that tree.'

For a few minutes nothing happened. Then, frightening her and making the horse team jump, Grogan took his shot. Instantly the "lumps" she'd been watching vanished. Ivan laughed.

'That was a small herd of antelope, resting in what shade that tree gave them. They'll run for a piece before hunting up some more shade. That's what they do, feed early and late and lie around all through the heat of the day. That's the way life should be lived, I think.'

Conversation between the two stalled soon after that. The horses kept their steady trot, stopping only when getting near enough to the river to be watered. At one point, Ivan brought up a small box containing sandwiches he'd purchased at the restaurant, and the two ate as the trip continued. Grogan took one and ate in the saddle.

The sun had started losing its heat and was getting close to the western mountains when, topping a rise, Russo pulled the team up and they sat for a moment looking down at a long valley below.

'That's the home place. Don't look like much from up here, but it's home.'

Still a distance away, but close enough for Susan to see he was right: it didn't look like much. Two stories, the main ranch

138

house stood in the center of a bare yard. A barn, which seemed to her to be leaning away, was a little farther along and on the left, while a series of long narrow sheds lined the yard on the other side. These, she figured, were the bunkhouses and probably the foreman's house.

Gigging the horses and slapping their rumps with the reins, Ivan got the team moving. As they drew nearer, Susan saw that the house had once been almost a mansion. Built of square-cut logs, a pair of big doors were centered in front behind a veranda that stretched from one corner to the other. Windows, deeply set into the walls in lines on either side of the front door. The glass panes in the upstairs windows caught the late-afternoon sun.

Without a word, Grogan rode off toward one of the narrow buildings on one side. Russo pulled the team to a halt, stepped on the near wheel and got down. Offering a hand, he helped Susan climb down. After sitting on the hard bench seat all day, both moved stiffly.

'Welcome to the Russo ranch,' he said, again laughing. 'We made better time than I figured. Probably should have taken a break somewhere along the way to work out the kinks.'

He took the handle of one of her smaller cases and motioned for her to go ahead up the steps. 'I'll bring the rest up in a little bit. Meanwhile, let's get you settled in so you can freshen up.'

Ivan led the way through one of the heavy wooden doors and headed straight for the broad curving stairway to one side of the entrance. Following behind, Susan didn't have time to inspect the interior, but her first impression was that the place needed more furniture and a good cleaning.

Upstairs, Ivan hurried along the hallway and went through a door toward the back of the house. On each side of the door, simple wooden benches lined the wall. The man stepped inside, placed her case on a large round table, turned to her and smiled.

'You'll find everything you need there.' He pointed toward a smaller door in the far wall. 'I'll be up to light the fire in a little while.'

A wide fireplace, she saw, took up one wall. On either side, heavy thick looking drapes hung on either side of the large many-paned windows. These, she thought, faced east and would be pleasant in the morning light. Now, with late afternoon shadows darkening the room, Susan felt her body tremble with a chill.

'Make yourself comfortable and I'll be back up after you've, uh, freshened up,' Ivan said, moving toward the door. Susan, standing near the table, turned in her assessment of the room and didn't see him go through the door. She heard the door close and spun around when she heard what sounded like a lock clicking. Quickly she stepped to the door, grabbed the doorknob and twisted. It didn't move. He had locked the door. She had been locked in.

CHAPTER 33

Shocked at finding herself a prisoner, Susan panicked and started beating the door with her fist. She was tired from the day's journey and now, shocked at Russo's action, tears began streaming down her cheeks before she could stop them. At last, holding the heel of one bruised hand in the other, she gave one last kick at the door with a booted toe. Then she stepped back and drew a deep breath.

Russo had locked her in. Leaning against the table, she closed her eyes and tried to calm down. Panic, she told herself, would not help. She had to think. Why had he done it? Where was his sister, or any other family members? Fear at the realization that she was all alone caused her to shiver. Holding herself tightly, she inhaled deeply and vowed silently not to cry. She would not give in.

Rather than stand there doing nothing, she looked around for a weapon. Other than a woven rug, which covered most of the floor and the fireplace, there was only the large wooden table for furniture in the room. Except for the thick wool drapes on each side of the twin windows, the room was bare. She ran to the little door set in the far wall, and found that it too was locked.

From one window the view was out over the roof of what she had thought would be the bunkhouse. Beyond that structure the land rolled away in undulating folds, soft and smooth

141

looking in the growing shadows. She caught sight of movement directly below and glanced down to see someone standing in front of the bunkhouse door. The foreman, Grogan, stood, hands on hips, looking up at her, smiling. The cold smile brought another chill of fear to her body.

She stepped quickly away from the window, and again hugging herself, she looked into the fireplace. Seeing it empty convinced her that the chill she'd felt had been caused by the cooling of the evening, not alarm.

The small case that Russo had brought up held little that would help her. Built into the bottom of the leather case was a traveling folding desk that contained pens, paper and an inkwell; the case itself held a few articles of clothing, a sweater, a short cape and her toilet kit. She took a sweater from it, and was slipping it on when she heard the key turn in the door.

She rushed round the table and stopped when Russo came into the room, carrying an armful of firewood. He looked at the young woman and smiled.

'It gets a little cool once the sun goes down,' he said. He locked the door and dropped the key in a pocket before going to the fireplace. 'I brought up enough wood to warm the room up and in a while I'll bring you some dinner. My apologies about the lack of chairs to sit on, but the upstairs doesn't get used very much any more.'

'Why are you doing this?' Susan asked, trying not to let the panic that was so close to overcoming her show in her voice. 'Where's your sister? Does she know you've got me locked up in here?'

'Well, no. You see I'm afraid there is no sister to tell,' he answered, still smiling. 'You could say I lied about that. Again, I apologize.' His smile clearly mocked her.

Quickly he laid a fire, touched a match to the kindling and watched for a moment as the wood blazed up.

'Why did you bring me here?' she asked, not really wanting to hear the expected answer. 'Why are you doing this to me?'

After making sure the wood he'd brought into the room was burning, and not answering her questions or even looking her way again, Russo went to the door, unlocked it and went out. Susan rushed to the door, getting her hand on the knob just as she heard the lock click once again.

As darkness filled the windows and warmth spread through the room, Susan found a place on the floor next to the fireplace. She sat down and leaned against the wall. Tired from the long day sitting on the bench seat of the swaying wagon, she felt herself relax.

CHAPTER 34

It was the sound of Russo kicking the door closed behind him that brought her awake. For a moment, she sat unmoving as she tried to figure out where she was. Remembering, she was on her feet in an instant, only to watch the man, holding a kerosene lantern in one hand, place a platter of sandwiches on the table.

'Had these left over from this morning,' he said, placing the lantern on the table. 'There isn't any reason for them to go to waste. Anyway, old Grogan and I aren't much good at cooking. Say, maybe while you're here you can take over that job; what do you say?' Again, his smile showed the mocking behind his words.

'No, I don't think I'd like cooking for either of you,' she answered, surprised at the firmness she heard in her words. 'Unless you've got a can of rat poison I could use to spice up the stew.'

'Ho, listen to you.' He laughed. 'A real firebrand, aren't you? Well, that's good. Having a simpering female on my hands won't get me what I want.' He pointed at the sandwiches, then turned to the door. As he unlocked it he looked back over one shoulder.

'Go ahead. Enjoy your supper. I'll be back up in a while and then we'll decide what to do with you.'

As soon as the door closed, Susan ran to it, making sure he

had locked it behind him.

Now with the light from the lantern on one side and the fireplace on the other, she sat on the floor and ate one of the sandwiches.

Susan couldn't tell how long it was before Russo come back into the room. After again carefully locking the door behind him and putting the key in a pocket, he walked over to the table. Susan moved away from him when he came close, stood up and went to the other side. Keeping the heavy wooden piece of furniture between them, she asked again why he was doing this to her.

'You've got what I want, but don't start thinking it has anything to do with you,' he sneered. 'At least, not yet.'

'I don't understand,' she said, frowning. They were standing one on each side of the round table, he leaning with both his hands flat on the surface, she with her arms folded over her chest. She would not, she swore to herself, show him how frightened she really was.

Light from the burning wood in the fireplace and the brighter, yellowish light of the lantern gave his angular face an evil cast. 'I've gone through your trunks and other things and what I want isn't there. Now I don't want to have to get rough, so it'd make things a lot easier if you'd just hand it over now.'

For a moment, she stood still, looking at him.

'I don't know what you mean. I don't have anything you'd want.'

'Yes. The way it worked out, you're the only one who could have it,' he said, moving a little to one side. Susan, watching closely, moved to keep the table between them.

'I don't know what you're talking about,' she said keeping her words low and even.

'At first we thought your old man had it. It had to come from either your pa or that other Californian rancher. When we didn't find it, well, that left only you, didn't it?' Russo said, moving back a step or two.

As if in some kind of slow dance, when the man moved a little one way, she moved the other, all the time watching him and shaking her head in denial.

'I tell you, I don't know what you're talking . . .' she started to say and then stopped. She stood very still. 'What do you mean, when you didn't find it? Was it you who searched my father's room?' Her face blanched at the next thought. Her voice trembled with shock as she asked the next question. 'What did you have to do with the murder of my father?'

'Oh, I didn't have anything to do with that. Why, I was, if you'll remember, busy helping the sheriff and that friend of his search for your pa. No, that was, I'm afraid, the work of my good foreman, Grogan.'

'Your foreman killed my father?' The shock of hearing him tell of the murder was made greater by his off-handed way of explaining it, as if he was just mentioning the time of day. Anger quickly over-shadowed the shock. He was going to pay for that, she vowed silently.

'We had been told that someone would be coming from the East to pick it up. Actually,' Russo said, letting one hand slide across the table as he stepped that way, 'Grogan was waiting in Denver, watching the man we'd been told would be the likely person. But somehow Grogan missed Kendrick with his little knife. I don't think I've ever seen Grogan miss with one of his knives. He didn't have another chance, so we waited until he got off the train there at Hunter's Crossing. When he didn't contact your pa, well, we had to do something to make sure they didn't have a chance to get together.'

Carefully matching his movement, Susan stared at the man. 'I still don't know what you're talking about.'

'Oh, it would have been so much easier if Grogan had been able to kill Kendrick before he got to Hunter's Crossing. That's what he was told to do, you know. Oh, don't look at me like that, it wasn't my idea. Naw,' he said, his smile looking to the young woman as if it were filled with evil. 'No, ma'am, it came from someone in Washington. Old Grogan fought in the war, you know. Pa didn't want me to go and, truth to tell, I didn't want any part of it. But Grogan's family was from somewhere outside of Richmond and he thought he'd better do what he could. Until the battle at Petersburg; that's when he came hurrying back here.'

As he talked, holding his eyes steadily on hers, he was moving slowly round the table. She matched him step for step. Chuckling softly, he went on talking.

'Well, it seems like one of the officers he'd served under was able to get a job up in Washington. All I know is, Grogan got a letter telling him it'd be worth his while to stop the messenger being sent West. The plan put out in that letter was for Grogan to kill Kendrick and take his place. It was a close thing, from what he told me. But somehow he missed. That Kendrick is one lucky man, I'd say.' He moved a step or two more, then he stopped and smiled his evil smile.

'Yes, that would have been easier. Grogan would have met your pa and we'd have had what we wanted. Nobody would have been hurt – well, except for Kendrick. But it didn't work out that way, did it? No. So, we had to find it ourselves. Your pa didn't have it on him like we thought he would, so we searched his room. When nothing was found there, we figured it had to be with that other old duck. He wasn't supposed to be in his room. He came in while Grogan was looking though his stuff, and, well, there was really nothing for my man to do, was there?' He held up his hands questioningly and moved another step or two.

Still directly across the table, Susan again shook her head. 'I still don't know what you're talking about,' she said, moving again as he did.

'Oh, I think you do. You're the only one who could have it, and I mean to take it. It's up to you how I go about getting it. I have to admit,' he said, looking at her slowly from her face downward, letting his eyes linger on her bosom. 'I'll enjoy finding it myself.'

Looking her in the face again, he went on, 'But that's up to you. Give it to me now, and I'll let you take the wagon and go. You can head back to Hunter's Crossing or even go on to Carson City if you'd like. It's up to you.'

'You think I'd trust you to keep your word and let me go?'

'Why not? Nobody would believe anything you told them. I'm just a poor rancher who gave you a ride and don't really understand why you decided to take off in the middle of the night. No, you give me what I want and you can go.'

'And I say I don't know what you mean. I don't have anything.'

'You may not know exactly what it is all about, but you've got it. I'll tell you so you'll know how important it is to us. It's a million dollars in gold. Ah, I see your eyes widen. You do know, don't you.' He smirked. 'It's gold your pa and a bunch of Californian businessmen got together. They are Union sympathizers and the gold was to go to help out the cash-strapped government. Well, that gold could help the South even more.' He stopped talking and moving when he saw Susan smile.

'You don't believe me?' He laughed. 'Maybe you're right. Well, some of the gold would stay with us, that's true. As it should. Think of it as a handling fee. But that's not all. No. That piece of paper you've got hidden somewhere not only tells when the gold is being shipped and how, but it's also a list of those businessmen. Think of it. With the gold, the South can finance another army. Gold can buy weapons in Europe and hire men to use them. And once the South rises up, those names on the list will be willing to pay anything to keep anyone from knowing who they are. You see, I don't need to keep all the gold. All I need is that paper you've got, and I mean to have it before you leave this room.'

CHAPTER 35

As they continued to move in their slow dance Susan felt the heat coming from the fireplace on her back.

'You are behind my father's death.' Her words were not a question, but a simple statement. For a moment she stood still, staring at the man across the table from her. His smile was answer enough.

Slowly Susan reached up and plucked at a thin gold chain that hung from her neck. Russo watched almost hypnotized as a small white enameled tube was pulled from her bodice. Holding it in one hand, she twisted the bottom. Then, her eyes not leaving his, she took a roll of thin white paper from the slender cylinder.

'Is this what you're looking for?' she asked, keeping her voice calm. 'Is this what he was murdered for?'

Russo's eyes lit up at sight of the paper. Moving with unsuspected speed, he was around the table in a rush. Susan stepped back and to one side and whipped the paper into the fireplace. He darted past her, shouting, his eyes never leaving the white flash. He reaching into the blaze, grabbed at the edge of the burning leaf and jerked it out, on to the floor. As he stomped to put the flames out, Susan reached the table and snatched up the first thing that came to hand, the lantern. Without thinking, she threw it at the man.

Her throw was wide, narrowly missing him as he bent over to

carefully pick up the tattered remains. Glass burst against the wall of the fireplace behind him. He looked up at the girl with eyes that now were crazed.

'Do you know what you've done,' he snarled.

Before she could react, a sheet of flame ignited the fuel oil that had sprayed across his back from the lantern. Instantly in pain, Russo threw himself backwards and into the draped window. Oil having splattered the drapes, they burst into flames with a whoosh. Susan stared as the blazing cloth seemed to envelop the now screaming man.

Seeing her chance at freedom, she whirled and ran to the door. The doorknob wouldn't turn. Glancing over one shoulder, she remembered him putting the key into a pocket as he'd entered the room. She coughed as smoke began to fill the room. Through the thick smoke she could see that the fire had spread to the other window drapery as well as the cloth rug. There was no sign of Russo, only a blackened bundle lying motionless on the floor on the far side of the table.

Beating on the door with her fists, she called out until the choking smoke silenced her cries for help.

CHAPTER 36

Jonathan had ridden the horse hard, until reason took over and he slowed to a steady trot. The smooth black shoulders of the animal were shiny in the mid-morning sunshine and white foam started dropping in clumps from his open mouth. Riding the horse into the ground, he realized, wouldn't help. Slowing even more, he rode on through the early afternoon. He stopped on the top of a small rise to let the horse breathe, and decided he'd have to take it even easier. For a mile or two he walked, leading the horse as it recovered from the early hard run.

Throughout the afternoon he walked and rode, hoping he was making better time than the wagon with Susan on board. Standing in the stirrups at every high point along the way, he strained his eyes, trying to catch a glimpse of the wagon. Only the tracks left in soft places told him he was still on the right trail.

The sun had gone behind the mountains to the west when he eventually came up over the ridge and looked down at the buildings. Lights filled a few windows with a soft orange color in the darkening evening. He sat for a minute, but saw no movement other than the thin thread of smoke coming from a chimney somewhere at the back of the main house. One window in a low building to the side was lit, all the rest of the spread was dark and still.

Seeing the wagon standing next to a pole corral, he squeezed his knees and gigged the horse into motion. He stopped at the wagon, tied the horse's reins to a wheel, pulled a Spencer rifle from its boot and levered a shell into the chamber. He'd looked just such a rifle over in the general store but, not having any money, could only look and dream. He twisted the tube magazine free and he saw that it was full. With one in the chamber, he had seven shots. Somehow he was going to have to find a way of thanking the owner of the brown mare for the loan of animal and the rifle.

'Well, well. Look who's here.' The words came out of the darkness behind him. Jonathan turned, brought the rifle up one-handed, then stopped. Standing where the gate in the fence should be was the big foreman, Grogan.

'Now what the hell do you think you're doing, boy?' Grogan asked, letting both his hands hang loosely at his sides. The smile, Jonathan saw in the dim light, wasn't welcoming. 'I wonder what you're planning, this late at night? There ain't no church here for you to give a sermon from.' The man laughed, sticking his right thumb in the edge of a pants pocket.

Jonathan, seeing the man wasn't wearing a gunbelt, relaxed a little and lowered the barrel of the rifle until it was pointing at the ground.

'I'm looking for Miss Harcourt,' he said, hoping his voice sounded firm and strong.

'You are, are you? Now why would you want her?'

'I'll tell her. Now, is she inside?' he asked, starting to turn away. At the young man's movement, Grogan's right hand came away from his pocket and Jonathan caught the flash of light as the man's arm came quickly up and forward, releasing the balanced throwing knife straight at the young man. Twice the knife spun in the air before the blunt solid end of its handle struck Jonathan squarely on the forehead, knocking him down.

Grogan walked over, shaking his head, to pick the knife off the ground next to the unconscious body.

152

'That's the first time I've misjudged the distance,' he murmured to himself. 'No,' he frowned, as he replaced the blade in its sheath, 'the second. The first time back there on the train and now this. Guess I need more practice.'

CHAPTER 37

Sheriff Blanchard and Kendrick had also ridden as fast as they could. Jonathan Neely was somewhere ahead of them and at every bend in the trail they half expected to find the young man and a dead horse, if not along the trail, then once they reached the Russo ranch. There they would get answers to why the rancher had lied about having a sister. Matt Kendrick had his own questions to ask.

All day they had held their horses to a steady trot. As dusk came on, making the shadows long, they were still a mile or so from the ranch when they saw the glow of a fire ahead. They kicked their mounts into a run and were flat out when, coming over the last ridge, they saw the back of the huge ranch house below, ablaze.

Blanchard pulled to a running halt in the ranch yard and swung out of the saddle. Seeing the dark form of a body, he ran to it. Matt jumped off his horse but didn't stop, pushing through the gate of the low dilapidated fence that ran along the front of the house. He rushed across the porch and slammed into the one of the double doors.

'Well, this is getting to be fun,' someone said behind him. Kendrick turned to look over his shoulder and saw Grogan standing next to the fence, his legs spread and hands on his hips. Instinctively he grabbed for his Colt, then stopped seeing that the foreman was unarmed.

154

'What's going on?'

'Now that's for the boss to figure out. You being here, though, gives me another chance to make things right. I missed the first time, but I won't now.' For the second time his right hand came up and forward, releasing the spinning blade directly at the big man's chest. Reacting to the movement, Kendrick completed his draw. He pulled the big Colt, in one motion thumbed back the hammer and with the barest twitch of a finger, fired.

The noise of the gun going off hid the sound of the knife slamming into the door, bare inches from where he'd been standing. Again, reacting without thought, Matt had fallen to one side, the knife missing by bare inches. Grogan's body, struck with the force of the .44 caliber bullet, had been flung back and he now lay without moving, flat on his back in the dirt.

Matt stood up and was reaching for the knife still stuck in the wood when he heard a terrifying scream from somewhere in the house. Not waiting, he threw his shoulder against one of the doors, slamming it open. He rushed into the entrance hall, then hesitated.

Unsure of where the scream came from, he was about to go farther into the house when he heard a muffled cry for help coming from upstairs. He took the stairway two steps at a time and didn't stop at the top but continued down the upper hallway. Banging sounds from the door at the far end stopped suddenly as he reached out for the doorknob. It wouldn't turn. Someone had locked it.

He heard another, weaker call for help and threw his shoulder against the door. It didn't move. A wooden bench was standing against a wall; he picked it up and swung it back, to use it as a battering ram. It hit the door just at the point of the lock, and the door sprung open.

Bellowing smoke poured out of the room upon a wave of blistering heat. Flames looked to fill the room as he took a cautious

155

step inside. With eyes streaming from the acrid smoke, he was about to turn away when he felt the toe of his boot strike something soft. Feeling blindly, he discovered it was a body he'd stumbled over.

He grabbed an arm and quickly backed out into the hallway, dragging the body. It was Susan and she was breathing. He picked her up, hurried down the hall and away from the burning room. Slowed by her unconscious weight and his smoke-filled lungs, he almost tripped over his own feet about halfway down the stairway. The loud sound of something behind him crashing through to the floor below made him move with uncommon speed.

He didn't stop to look around, but used an elbow to push open the front door. Then he half-ran, half-fell down the walk and, careful not to trip over the dead foreman's body, sped away from the house.

As he gently set her down he felt her cough and choke as her lungs spewed up the smoke they'd taken in. He loosened the collar of her dress and he brushed her long black hair from her face.

'Breathe easy, Miss Harcourt. You're safe now,' he said softly. He turned to look at the house, now fully in flames, and heard, as if from a great distance, someone call. He reached for his holstered Colt and felt an empty scabbard. He had left his revolver behind in the burning house; he was weaponless and light-headed from the smoke that had filled his lungs. Whoever was coming was going to catch both of them helpless and there wasn't anything he could do about it.

CHAPTER 38

'Well, if that don't take the cake,' Sheriff Blanchard said, kneeling on one knee on the other side of the woman, 'I find young Neely unconscious in the yard and you go traipsing into a burning building. From the looks of things, it's a good thing we got here when we did. Are you all right, Susan?'

'Yes,' her voice sounded weak and raspy, 'thanks to Mr Kendrick here. It was wonderful, when he smashed down the door. I was sure I'd never get out of that room.'

Blanchard nodded and looked over at Matt. 'What was that shooting I heard a while ago?'

'The foreman, Grogan,' Matt answered, pointing toward the smoldering pile that had been the big ranch house. 'His body is over there.'

'What the hell?' the sheriff said in surprise. He looked down at the girl and shook his head. 'Excuse my language, Susan, but Jonathan said Grogan had tried to kill him and now Matt says that's who he shot. What's going on?'

'That's OK, Sheriff.' She smiled tiredly. 'I'm glad he's dead. His boss, Russo, is dead too,' she said. Ignoring his question, she look up past Kendrick's shoulder and smiled.

'Miss Harcourt,' Jonathan Neely said, walked up a little unsteady on his feet, 'are you all right?'

'Yes. Thanks to Mr Kendrick. Sheriff Blanchard said Grogan tried to kill you. Are you OK?'

157

'Yes, he hit me on the head with something and I have a headache, but I'm OK. But I don't understand what this was all about. Did that Russo think he'd get away with kidnapping you, Susan?'

'No. Russo wasn't after me. What he really wanted was to get me and my things somewhere out of town.'

'What was he after?' the sheriff asked quietly

'It's a long story, Sheriff. I guess I'd better explain. My father and his friends wanted to send gold east to Washington. There was a message that he was to give to someone.' She stopped and looked over at where Matt was sitting. 'He never told me who that would be. It was you, I believe, Mr Kendrick.'

Sheriff Blanchard glanced his way. 'So that's what you're doing here. I couldn't figure that out.'

Matt simply nodded. 'Yes. But I hadn't been told who would have it. I suppose that's why your pa and that other rancher were killed?'

'Yes. Father had given the paper to me to keep safe, and when they were killed, I felt I should get back to let them know that the message hadn't gotten through. Our new governor is one of the men who were involved. Russo had somehow learned about the gold and he wanted it for himself.'

Slowly, taking her time and answering those questions that she could, she told the men what Russo had told her. Kendrick could only frown when she told about throwing the piece of paper into the fireplace.

After taking care of the horses and finding enough bedding in the bunkhouse, the four of them spent the rest of the night in some comfort.

The next morning, after a breakfast of water from the well, they headed back toward Hunter's Crossing. Matt and the sheriff had dug a shallow grave for Grogan. Matt ran his thumb across the thin blade of the man's throwing knife, nodded and slipped the blade inside the top of his boot. A quick search through the pile of scorched timbers and ash, all that was left of the big house, didn't turn up any sign of Russo. His body, Sheriff Blanchard figured from what Susan had said, had probably been totally consumed by the fire.

Riding side by side, the two men rode out ahead of the wagon. Susan and Jonathan seemed quite content to drive the wagon back, somehow falling behind the two men on their rested horses.

'I wouldn't wonder if you've got another battle coming up with your good friend, the Reverend Caleb Neely,' Matt said, glancing back over his shoulder.

Blanchard followed the direction of his look and smiled. 'Yeah, well it seems to me that Susan has more need for the preacher's boy that his pa does. I never did think Jonathan was likely to follow in his pa's footsteps. And that Susan is a good person who's all alone now. From what I'd guess is being talked about back there, they might be working things out that'll be for the best.'

Although hungry and a little out of sorts about not having had his morning coffee, Sheriff Blanchard felt pretty good. 'You know, I think when we get back into town and I explain to the circuit judge who was really behind those killings, it might be time for me to hand in this badge. I wasn't cut out for that; trying to please the folks who hired me and at the same time keep all the outsiders happy.'

He glanced at Matt and he smiled. 'That'd leave the job wide open for some enterprising young man. I happen to know of one,' he went on, not giving the other man an opening, 'one who, while not a Pinkerton detective, is a retired army officer. Why, without a doubt I bet you could get hired as quick as I could get this badge off me.'

Kendrick laughed. 'No, I'm afraid that isn't for me. There's still the matter of the gold shipment that I was to find out about. I think I'll wait around until the train is running again and then travel on over to meet up with those California business men.

With Miss Susan's introduction, maybe I can get the information that the good Colonel Cummings wanted. And after that's taken care of, I'll start looking for what I want to get into. Her pa and old Joad Howard might have had the right idea about raising cattle.'

'Well, if you get over there and change your mind, this country can always use a good man.'

Jonathan Neely wasn't giving much thought to having missed breakfast or even to what his father was going to say. He was sitting comfortably beside the California girl on the wagon and had things to think about other than food, coffee or the hardness of the wagon seat. Even the facts that he didn't have a job, a place to hang his hat or even a horse to call his own, could not stop the smile that now seemed to be plastered permanently to his face.

The ranch over near the American River, Susan Harcourt thought, would need someone with strength to help her keep it successful. Her father had never faltered in his dreams and she was, after all, her father's daughter. Somehow she felt, this young man beside her would probably work out quite well.